Christmas Calling

Two Heartwarming Christmas Novellas
best selling authors
Colleen L. Reece and Birdie Etchison

Christmas Challenge

by Colleen L. Reece

Colleen L. Reece learned to read by kerosene lamplight in a home without running water or electricity, but rich in love for God and Family. The kitchen and dining room were once a one-room school house where Colleen's mother taught all eight grades. The former cloakroom was Colleen's bedroom. There she dreamed of someday writing a book.

A logger's daughter, Colleen considers herself an ordinary person with an extraordinary God. He has multiplied her 'someday book' into 150 "Books you can trust". Six million copies have sold.

Colleen launched Barbour Publishing Romance Readers Flip Books and Barbour's *Heartsongs Presents* book club. Twice voted favorite author and inducted in the Hall of Fame, several of Colleen's books have appeared on the CBA Bestseller list.

Chapter One

What now, Lord?

Valerie Shannon O'Shea stared out the window of her home above Lake Michigan, feeling as battered as the shore below. The weeks since her guardian for the past ten years was laid to rest seemed like a lifetime. Her future loomed even more colorless than the late spring day outside. Rain had beaten down the few flowers bold enough to poke their heads out of the hard ground and shiver in the cold. A small boat, torn free from its moorings, tossed on the churning waters.

Just like me, Valerie thought. *Alone and adrift.*

The mantel clock tolled off eleven ponderous strokes. Valerie sighed and turned from the window, thankful for the cheerful yellow walls and bright rugs. Cuddled in the plushy embrace of her favorite chair, she opened her well-used Bible. She turned the pages and read at random until she reached Isaiah 65:24: *And it shall come to pass, that before they call, I will answer; and while they are yet speaking, I will hear.*

A lump rose to her throat and she clutched the Bible close to her heart. "Lord, I need Your help. I'm desperate. Mr. Harper's nephew takes possession of the house soon." She closed her eyes. Money wasn't a problem yet, but it soon would be.

She wasn't established enough as an artist to make a living yet. And the anonymous, monthly bank drafts marked for *Shannon O'Shea* that had arrived for several years after she came to Chicago had suddenly stopped when she turned twenty-one. Of course, she had never wanted to rely on those checks since she had no idea who they were from in the first place.

If only Da . . .

Valerie flinched. The worst day of her life came to mind: Whitewind, Montana, near Missoula. Her father condemned to prison for a crime he swore he didn't commit. Looking into Danny O'Shea's lake-blue eyes so like her own, Valerie had vowed to seek justice.

News came of her father's death just before Christmas that same year—a few months after her guardian brought her to Chicago. It deepened her resolve. She would clear Da's name, no matter how long it took or how high the cost.

"Lord, that's why I've worked so hard to sell my paintings," she mused. "And saved everything I could from the money they brought, but it isn't enough."

Trust Me.

Valerie started and sprang from her chair. "Who...?"

The only sound in the quiet room came from the muted cry of gulls driven shoreward because of the storm. Warmth flowed into Valerie's chilled heart. The same God who cared for fallen sparrows would care for her.

A knock on the door interrupted her thoughts. "Miss O'Shea?"

Valerie ran to open the door. "Come in, Mrs. Gregory. What are you doing out on this miserable day?"

Her closest neighbor shook her head and held out a newspaper-wrapped bundle for Valeria. "I can't stay. Supper's waiting at home, but I brought you a piece of johnnycake."

Heedless of her friend's wet coat, Valerie hugged her. "Thank you so much."

"Think nothing of it. That's what neighbors are for." Mrs. Gregory, a dumpling of a woman, splashed her way back down the steps and to her own house.

A fresh wave of loneliness washed over Valerie. Losing her guardian and the home she loved was bad enough. Losing Mrs. Gregory, the closest thing to a mother Valerie had ever known, was worse.

She watched until her friend entered the house next door, then she carried the package to the kitchen and removed the newspaper and a tea towel.

"Mmm, still warm, and it smells heavenly." For the first time since the funeral, she felt like eating.

Leaving the newspaper on the table, Valerie made short work of the generous chunk of johnnycake and finished with a tall glass of milk.

Refreshed, she started to crumple the newspaper, but then paused. Bold headlines at the top of the front page of the *Chicago Tribune* caught her attention.

IS THE PIONEER SPIRIT STILL ALIVE AND WELL?

The sub-heading read:

*Local financier challenges young women
of our fair city to prove themselves.*

"What on earth . . . ?" Valerie smoothed the paper and read on.

*Train fare to Missoula, Montana,
and a substantial cash prize will be awarded
to a Chicago woman (at least 21 years old) daring enough
to reside in a former one-room schoolhouse for a full year.
No modern conveniences. Candidate must prove herself as
resourceful as the early settlers' wives and daughters.
Failure to comply with the stated rules will cancel
both the prize and return fare.*

*Any young woman willing to adapt Horace Greeley's
famous advice to "Go West, young man, and grow up with
the country" should apply in care of this newspaper.*

Valerie gulped and read the column again. Her heart leaped to her throat. Coincidence? The challenge, coming by way of a crumpled newspaper, appeared to be Providential. Otherwise, why would they choose *Missoula*, of all places?

. . . before they call, I will answer . . . while they are yet speaking, I will hear.

Valerie fell to her knees. "Lord, if this challenge is really Your will for me, please open the way." Pain lanced through her. "Even though it means going back to where Da and I had happy times, especially at Christmas," she murmured. A river of memories suddenly flooded her mind.

The fragrance of freshly cut Christmas trees and cedar boughs. Scarlet ribbons on brown paper packages. Laughing at Da when they made angels in the snow. The Christmas Eve service in the little community church at Whitewind. Snowball fights and sleigh rides. Gone forever.

Christmas in Chicago had been far different. Valerie had tried to keep cheerful for her guardian's sake, but after her father's death it was almost impossible.

Now she wondered. Would the challenge of spending Christmas in an abandoned schoolhouse, even if she was able to clear her father's name, be too hard? Valerie waited for the pain to subside then continued to pray, "Lord, I vowed to do whatever it took, no matter how high the cost to clear my father's name. I am committed to doing just that, but I need You to go with me."

Peace and the assurance her Heavenly Father would never leave her alone stole into Valerie's troubled heart, only to be pushed aside by a new fear.

Valerie sprang to her feet and peered at the newspaper once more.

How old was the *Tribune* article?

Chapter Two

"Thank You, God. Surely, few young women will have braved the storms to answer this advertisement!"

She firmed her lips, donned weatherproof clothing, and hurried out. When the door closed behind her, she felt it marked the end of an era; the beginning of a new life.

Forty-five minutes later Valerie stared into the steely gray eyes of the man who held her future in his ink-stained hands. She swallowed the flutter in her throat and gave him back glance for glance. Danny O'Shea's daughter bowed to no man.

"What makes you think you can survive in the wilds of Montana?" Mr. Stone challenged. "You don't look like a pioneer."

Stone by name, stone of face. Valerie disciplined a smile and said, "Looks can be deceiving, sir. I come from sturdy stock."

He snorted and raised a disbelieving eyebrow.

Valerie didn't wait for him to argue. "I was raised with little. My parents came across the Atlantic on a coffin boat to escape the Irish Potato Famine. Things still weren't easy; we had to be frugal. After my mother died, Da and I traveled West."

Mr. Stone cocked his head and looked suspicious. "Where in the west?"

She clenched her sweating hands and swallowed again. "Montana."

He made a rude noise. "So, you are looking for free transportation to your old home?"

Please, God, help me know how to answer this man correctly.

"Well?"

"No. I have three reasons, but a free ride is not one of them." She began to tick them off on gloved fingers. "One, to prove I am as good as our pioneer women."

Stone crossed his arms and glared. "It won't be easy. The man making the offer is convinced that modern women are little more than husband-hunters armed with pretty faces and fancy clothes. He believes whoever is chosen will fail and is putting up the money to prove he's right." Stone's mouth turned down. "He usually is."

Valerie tilted her chin. "This time he needs to be proved wrong."

The glimmer of a smile crossed Mr. Stone's face, so fleeting she wondered if it had really been there. "Your other reasons are . . . ?"

"I want to paint the Montana mountains, lakes, and meadows."

Mr. Stone leaned forward. He seemed interested but at the same time he looked ready to pounce. "And the third reason?"

She shot a silent prayer up. This was the most important reason.

Valerie clasped her hands and looked Mr. Stone square in the eyes. There was no point in beating around the bush, she needed to tell him the truth. "I want to clear my father's name. He died in prison for a crime he didn't commit."

"How do you know he didn't commit it?" The man looked doubtful.

Valerie was used to that response. No one ever believed her.

Valerie felt her lips curve up. "If you had known Danny O'Shea, you wouldn't ask that question."

Her hands clenched. Had she gone too far?

Apparently not. Mr. Stone tilted his chair back until it squeaked and said, "Well, at least you've got spunk. And from what you've shared with me, I can tell that you are honest." His mouth twitched, and he snatched up a packet of pages. "Now about the rules—"

"I'm accepted?" Valerie squeaked.

A wide grin changed Stoneface into a completely different person.

"Anyone brave enough to come out in this kind of weather to answer an ad for such a harebrained idea should be able to handle western Montana for a year."

Valerie looked relieved, but her insides still trembled.

Mr. Stone harrumphed. "I see one obstacle. Won't people out there remember you?"

Valerie shook her head. "I don't think so. I was a gawky fourteen-year-old known as Shannon O'Shea. Now I will be Valerie Shannon, the name with which I sign my paintings. There's no reason for anyone to suspect I am there for any other reason except to capture the Montana scenery on canvas and prove that a modern woman can live as a pioneer."

Mr. Stone stood and held out his hand with a look of admiration on his face.

"Godspeed, Miss O'Shea." A wistful look crept into his eyes. "I envy you. If I didn't have a wife and a passel of kids to feed I'd love to homestead in Montana—even if it meant living in an abandoned schoolhouse."

Valerie managed to grip his hand, thank him, and then she stumbled out of the office and into the hall.

She collapsed against a wall and began to giggle. "Lord, looks really *are* deceiving. Who would believe a newspaper man like Mr. Stone would hanker to be a homesteader in Montana?" Then she grew serious. "Thank you, Lord for allowing me to be chosen."

In the days that followed, Valerie had reason to thank God for Mr. Stone several times. Obviously wanting her to succeed and justify his choice, he insisted that she memorize the many rules.

He also warned, "The financier behind this unique adventure has connections with persons in Missoula. They will keep a close eye on you. Frankly, they are also skeptical that any woman today can meet and handle the test." A smile showed in his watchful eyes. "Don't let me down, Miss O'Shea. And don't back out in the middle of the challenge and marry some Montana cowboy."

I only know one Montana cowboy worth considering, Valerie thought with a huff, *and he's surely married by now. Besides, his da sent my da to prison! I don't dare tell Mr. Stone that. It might kill the only opportunity I ever have to bring about long-delayed justice.*

Valerie had assured Mr. Stone that she would not back out of the challenge. Clearing her father's name and becoming an established painter meant too much to her. Marriage was the last thing on her mind.

*****

On June first, Valerie boarded the westbound train. The mournful *woohoo* of the whistle dinned in her ears, followed by the *clackety-clack* of turning wheels.

Valerie sat watching as the scenery outside of the train window changed as they moved out of the city. She swallowed a boulder-sized lump in her throat and didn't look back.

Regardless of what lay ahead, Valerie knew in her heart Chicago would never again be home.

Chapter Three

Every *clackety-clack* of the train wheels that carried Valerie Shannon from Chicago to Montana plunged her into the past. Memories crept in while she watched the scenery change outside the window.

She tried to brush them away, unwilling to face the bittersweet and often painful scenes that flashed through her mind.

Before she knew it, she was in Montana and riding in a buckboard towards her new home. Each step of the plodding team that took her and her belongings from Whitewind to the old schoolhouse brought back a flood of memories. Was this how Rip Van Winkle felt when he awakened from his long sleep?

The driver, who said his name was Charley, shifted the quid in his cheek and expertly sent a stream of tobacco juice between his mules' ears. "Do you really aim to live in that old schoolhouse?" The doubt in his voice sent shivers down Valerie's spine.

"I do."

The grizzled man guffawed. "'pears to me it's more likely you'll be saying those words in a church afore the year's up."

Valerie shook her head in defense, tired of everyone assuming that she would be considering getting married.

"Plenty of young bucks around here will come courting."

Valerie smiled at him and shook her head. "I will not be getting married for a long time and I doubt I will have much time for courting. I think that living alone in the schoolhouse will be enough for me."

Charley scratched his balding head with a bony finger. "You'll change your mind when the men start calling. Maybe even Locke Stuart will come around, although he ain't one for trailing the ladies. Never has been."

Charley's comment brought Valerie upright on the seat and robbed her of speech. So, Locke had never been one for 'trailing the ladies'? Was it possible . . . No, if he had cared about her, he would have answered her letters.

The driver rambled on unaware of the thoughts flooding Valerie's mind. "Locke always was a mighty fine boy. Too bad his daddy favored Locke's older brother." Charley snorted. "Never did cotton to Jed. I don't trust a man who won't look you square in the eyes." He glanced both ways as if to make sure no one lurked alongside the dusty wagon track within hearing range. "Long about ten year ago, as I recall, just afore Jed up and disappeared, there was some funny business on the Lucky L."

Valerie felt as if she'd been struck by lightning. She turned her head sharply and stared at the man. "Funny business? What do you mean?"

"Well, Judge Stuart sent a man to prison for stealing. I always wondered if he hadn't convicted the wrong man."

Valerie feigned interest now and asked casually, "What was the man's name?"

"Danny O'Shea. Well-liked. Full of fun, but a God-fearing man, or so everyone thought." Charley looked wise. "A lot of folks around here still think so. I always wondered if Jed had something to do with the funny business, and O'Shea covered up for him."

"Do you really think so?" Valerie's heart was pounding with excitement.

Charley nodded slowly. "Only thing, why would he do that? O'Shea had a motherless daughter who thought the sun rose and set in him. Why would he allow himself to go to prison when she needed him?"

Just then the wagon hit a chuckhole jarring them both. Valerie clutched the seat and took a deep breath. What if Jed Stuart had been guilty and Da took the blame? Preposterous! Yet quixotic as it appeared, it was the kind of thing Da would do.

Just like Jesus.

The words brought blood singing in Valerie's ears. She'd never had an inkling of what really happened except knowing Da was no thief. Now, Charley's monologue gave her something to consider, something to hope for.

She started to pump him for more information but refrained. A stranger showing undue interest would surely arouse suspicion in anyone as observant as her driver and she had already asked several questions. She decided to change the subject.

"What is the schoolhouse like?" she inquired.

Charley cackled. "Not a lot to tell. You seen one, you seen 'em all. 'Cept you're in luck. You won't have to pack water. The school board and parents dug a shallow well and put in a pump when the school was built. The pump's outside, but it's a heap better than depending on the creek for water. 'Specially in winter."

Valerie gave a sigh of relief. "That's a blessing." She shivered in spite of the warm day. "Having to break ice to get water was one of my biggest concerns."

Several other thoughts flashed through her mind. There were many things that concerned her about the choice she had made in coming to Montana.

"It still ain't gonna be easy," Charley warned. "You're gonna have to cut wood between now and winter to carry you through." He coughed. "Me and some of the boys from the Lucky L will be glad to stop by and help you."

His offer made Valerie choke up. "Thanks, Charley, but part of the deal is that I have to do this completely on my own. I'm strong. Besides, I've chopped plenty of wood before."

He turned his head from the slow-moving pair of mules and stared at her in obvious disbelief. "A Chicago gal cut wood?"

Valerie gulped. "I didn't always live in Chicago."

Charley's eyes filled with questions.

She frantically continued on. "Tell me about the folks around here." Thankfully, Charley didn't ask questions that might give away her identity and real mission.

*****

A week later Valerie surveyed her new home. She mentally checked off what she had accomplished on her own.

Pump primed with creek water and performing well. Old stove blackened and in good working order. Outhouse free of spiders that had fled before an onslaught of boiling water and lye soap. A pile of wood stacked next to the building. Walls, windows, and floor scrubbed. Cot neatly made with bedding from home. A few of her paintings and sunny yellow calico curtains brightened the room. Blisters had given way to calluses.

Her only visitor so far had been Dusty Devlin, a cowboy from the Lucky L. Valerie had burned to question him all about the Stuarts but wisely kept still.

Now, she sank to her cot. Satisfaction for a job well done gave way to exhaustion. So far she had met the challenges, but they had taken a toll. Too tired to even wash her face, she sank to her cot.

Minutes or hours later, a thunderous knock and a horse neighing yanked Valerie from a deep sleep. She roused enough to stumble to the window. From the shelter of the curtain, she peered out at the tall man who stood on her porch. A broad-brimmed Stetson hid his face.

Valerie's heart sank. Dusty Devlin had been pleasant and polite, but why did he have to come calling now? All she wanted to do was sleep.

Tempted to ignore him, she stifled a yawn and opened the door. "Yes?"

Chapter Four

Judge Stuart glared at his youngest son from under thick white eyebrows. He bent an ivory letter opener back and forth in his strong fingers. It boded ill for the cowboy slumped in a chair across the desk of the lavishly furnished Missoula office. "When are you going to marry one of the young women around here and give me a grandson?" he demanded. "It's time you settled down."

Only the commandment to honor father and mother kept Locke from telling the judge to mind his own business. He gritted his teeth and retorted, "Don't count on it. I have no time for a wife. The Lucky L keeps me busy twenty-four hours a day." *Besides, only one girl has ever made my heart pound,* he silently added, *and she's long gone.*

Locke sprang from his comfortable chair before the floodgates to a river of memories broke open. He headed for the door.

The letter opener broke with a loud *snap.* Then an obviously reluctant smile softened the lines of the judge's craggy face.

"Not many twenty-eight-year-old men own their own ranch," he gloated. "Even if you were uglier than sin—which you aren't—you'd still be Whitewind's most eligible bachelor."

Locke spun on his heel and glared at his father. He clenched his fists. "Think I want a wife who marries me for the ranch? Mother didn't marry *you* for what you owned."

The judge fitted his fingertips together and shrugged. "That's 'cause I didn't have anything when we met. It all came later."

Locke couldn't help grinning. "Right." He cocked his head and suggested, "Maybe Jed will come home with a wife and kids."

An unreadable expression crossed the judge's face. "Not likely. I'm afraid in this case the *older* brother is the prodigal son."

Locke bit his lip, wishing he had remained silent. Jed had always been their father's favorite. As dark-haired and wild as Locke was blond and tractable, Jed's unexplained disappearance years before had changed his father beyond belief. Within a few months of Jed's leaving, the judge's gray hair turned pure white.

Sympathy overrode Locke's irritation at being badgered. "Don't give up on me, Dad. If ever the right woman comes along, you may get a grandchild after all." He laughed. Ignoring his father's *harrumph*, Locke turned around and strode determinedly out the door.

Hours later, Locke and his favorite horse, Lariat, topped a rise on the far reaches of the Lucky L. It felt good to be away from Missoula and the judge's nagging.

Locke doffed his Stetson and wiped sweat from his forehead. "Getting warm for mid-June." He patted the bay's neck and breathed in the pungent smell of sage. Lariat snorted and danced sideways.

"What's spooking you?" Locke asked, peering down at a stand of trees.

A heartbeat later, he froze in the saddle. Lazy tendrils of smoke rose from the midst of the close-growing trees. An acrid odor assaulted Locke's nostrils.

Blood rushed to his head. Dread filled him. Smoke coming from the old, abandoned schoolhouse by the creek spelled trouble. Trouble and danger. It only took one spark to start a range fire, the scourge of Montana and the Lucky L. Locke had once been forced to ride a horse to death then stumble on foot in order to escape the wind-driven flames. If he hadn't reached the river . . .

Remembering sent him into a cold sweat. He would never forget his prayer of thankfulness when he plunged into the water. Shoulders burned from hot ash, he stayed under until his lungs felt they would burst. Time after time he came up just long enough to breathe then went down again, barely conscious of wild animals swimming around him and seeking escape.

Now, Locke leaned forward and hollered "giddup!" in Lariat's ear. His mind outdistanced his horse while they pelted down the gentle slope. Apprehension and rage filled him.

Who or what would he find? Outlaw? Tramp? Locke gritted his teeth. Whoever it was had better have a good reason for ignoring the *No Trespassing* sign posted on the old schoolhouse door. A mighty good reason.

Chapter Five

Locke reined Lariat in a few yards from the old schoolhouse and wheeled when the steady drumbeat of horses' hooves sounded behind him.

"Hey, Locke!" came a raucous yell. "You gonna call on the pretty little filly livin' in the schoolhouse?" Dusty Devlin, Locke's favorite cowboy, and one known on the Lucky L for his love of mischief, brought his buckskin to a screeching halt and grinned at his boss.

"What are you talking about?" Locke demanded.

Dusty shoved his worn Stetson back on his curly red hair and drawled. "Where you been? Stuck with your head in a gopher hole? The best-lookin' gal to blow into these parts for years done took up residence over yonder more'n a week ago." He pointed to the old schoolhouse a short distance away. "If you don't believe me, take a gander at them winders."

Locke glanced at the shining clean windows on either side of the plank door, then snorted. "That doesn't mean anything. If this isn't one of your tall tales, I'm a ring-tailed raccoon."

Dusty's eyes gleamed. "It's the truth, so help me. I hear tell some Chicago bigwig figgered no gal today could live like our pioneer ancestors. He put out a mighty sweet deal in the city newspaper."

"What was it?"

"Any young woman who can live out here for a year without help from anyone gets a big ree-ward for puttin' up with heat, hail, snow, and whatever."

"The fella must be crazy! No woman would take up such an offer. Probably some tramp or squatter's making himself at home."

Dusty chuckled. "How many tramps and squatters wash winders or hang yaller curtains and scrub porch floors? This one ain't got a dead leaf or piece of dry grass on it. I suggest, all respekful like, that you go knock on the door and find out who's livin' here." A devilish laugh followed. "Better brace yourself, boss."

Convinced this was just one of Dusty's tricks, Locke leaped from Lariat and strode toward the building. His boot heels resounded on the shallow steps and across the small, covered porch. Feeling like a fool for even considering Dusty might for once be telling the truth, Locke thumped on the weathered door.

A whisper of sound came from within. It feathered along Locke's veins, leaving him feeling like he stood on the brink of something important. *Ridiculous.* Why should the prospect of meeting some tramp or squatter leave him breathless?

The door swung inward. "Yes?"

Locke's mouth dried to a crisp. His heart stilled then thundered until it threatened to choke him. *What? Who?*

His mind refused to accept what his eyes beheld. Dusty was right. No tramp or squatter occupied the old schoolhouse. A young woman fair enough to turn the head of any man stood before him. Curly black hair cascaded to the shoulders of a blue-checked gown. Pansy-blue eyes stared at him from a dust-streaked face, unlike any eyes Locke had seen in ten years. He tried three times before he could speak. When he did, it was barely above a whisper. "Shan —"

Dismay crept into the girl's face and choked off Locke's exclamation. One hand flew to her heart and she turned chalk-white. Locke reeled. But before he could start asking the multitude of questions galloping through his mind, Dusty came up beside him.

"Miss Shannon, make Mr. Locke Stuart's acquaintance. He's boss of the Lucky L." The man did not seem to notice the shocked expression on both faces. "Locke, say howdy to Miss Valerie Shannon. She aims to win herself a grubstake by livin' out here all by her lonesome and paintin' up a storm." Dusty doffed his hat. "She showed me a few of her pictures a coupla days ago when I just happened to stop by. If they're a sample, folks around here will be standin' in line to buy 'em."

The cowboy's honest admiration brought color back to the girl's face, but Locke glared at Dusty. So, he had just *happened* to stop by. Not likely. A twinge of jealousy gnawed at Locke's vitals. He squashed it, far more concerned with the name change than with Dusty's ramblings.

Valerie Shannon? No! Ten years had merely increased Locke's first and only love's beauty. He had thought he'd die from pain at age eighteen, when Shannon O'Shea vanished after her father's trial and conviction. He had waited years for a letter. None came, but Locke never forgot her.

Now, he set his jaw. *I lost her once. I won't again. Before I let that happen, I'll toss her on Lariat's saddle, ride off, and marry her.*

Chapter Six

Valerie opened the schoolhouse door and felt the blood drain from her face. There stood Locke Stuart, frowning at her. All the way from Chicago to Whitewind she had feared meeting him, but wondered about him at the same time. What kind of man would the boy she had adored ten years earlier become?

She never dreamed their first meeting would be like this. Conscious of her disheveled appearance, one hand flew to her hair in a vain attempt to smooth it. She could think of nothing to say.

Locke's face went chalk-white. He whispered, "Shan—"

Valerie clutched the door frame for support. Panic tightened her fingers until they ached, and she sent Locke an imploring glance. Her shoulders drooped. She hadn't counted on being recognized so soon.

Dusty stepped forward and broke into the awkward moment. He removed his Stetson. "Good to see you again, Miss. This here's Mr. Locke Stuart, boss of the Lucky L. Locke, make Miss Valerie Shannon's acquaintance."

Dusty rattled on with small talk, but Valerie tuned him out and fixed her gaze on Locke's face.

The years have been kind to him, she mused. The broad shoulders, golden hair, and blue eyes she remembered so well remained the same. Other than a few crinkles around his eyes that attested to long hours in the Montana sun, Locke was merely an older version of the boy who had stolen her fourteen-year-old heart.

Now, her heart skipped a beat. The set of Locke's jaw boded no good for a deceiver. Why had she ever embarked on this crazy journey? For one cowardly moment she wished she could hop on the first train back to Chicago, but then she stood straight.

There is nothing to go back to, even if I had train fare.

Locke's penetrating gaze never left her face. "May we come in, Miss . . . *Shannon*?"

Valerie silently stood aside and watched him enter. *Say something*, she admonished–herself. *Anything to break this awful tension! It's thick enough to cut with a dull saw.*

Dusty must have felt it. He shuffled his feet and mumbled, "I'll go water the horses, Locke." He headed back into the yard.

Valerie dropped into a chair she'd made from a packing box and had covered with yellow calico that matched the curtains.

Locke towered over her, arms crossed and forbidding. "Dusty told me a wild yarn about a woman foolish enough to think she could win a bet by living here for a year. So, Miss Valerie Shannon O'Shea, what's the *real* story?"

She searched his face for a sign of softening but found none. "I…I… my guardian died. I had nowhere else to go."

He raised a skeptical eyebrow. "So?"

"So, I took the offer. My paintings have been selling, but I'm not yet established enough to make a living. I wanted new scenery for my paintings. There are plenty of wonderful things to paint here."

"That's the *whole* reason?" His gaze bored into her.

The desire to shake him out of his maddening calm—when what she really wanted was to fling herself into his arms and cry on his shoulder—threw caution to the winds. "I came back to prove Da innocent of the charge that sent him to prison." She sprang up, planted her fists on her hips, and glared. "You may as well know. Not you or Judge Stuart or anyone else is going to keep me from clearing Danny O'Shea's name!"

A slow smile crept across Locke's tanned face.

The poignant light she remembered so well filled his eyes. "Would you like some help?"

It proved her undoing. She dropped back to her chair, covered her face with her hands, and began to cry all the tears she'd been holding back for years.

A moment later, a strong hand gently touched her hair. "I'm glad you came." A pause. "Shannon, why didn't you answer my letters?"

Valerie raised her head and gasped. "Letters? I received no letters, even though I wrote to you for a full year. I thought you had forgotten me."

Locke's smile died. "Never." His face darkened. "Clearly, somebody intercepted those letters. I'm going to find out who . . . and why."

The honorable, Judge Stuart, who may not be so honorable, she thought.

"You really wrote?" she looked up at him with hope in her eyes.

"Yes."

Regret filled each of them, but there was nothing that they could do about it now. Too many years had passed. They had no common ground between them any longer.

Locke turned away, trying to make sense of the situation.

Valerie's eyes filled with tears, but she blinked them back. The unspoken words pounded in her mind until Locke broke the silence and said, "Finding out the truth about your father won't be easy. I know. I tried. I even visited your father in prison, but he only repeated he had never stolen anything. I believed him then and I believe him now. I wondered if he was covering up for someone-"

Valerie gave a startled cry, surprised at Locke's words.

"Hey, Boss," Dusty interrupted from the porch. "If we're gonna check the herd in the south pasture, we'd best be moseyin' along."

Valerie smothered the words, *that's what Charley said about Da.* Until God and now Locke helped her establish Da's innocence, unfounded accusations were best kept to herself.

"Coming, Dusty!" Locke called over his shoulder.

Valerie gave him a smile with trembling lips.

He took Valerie's hands in his range-hardened ones. "I've gotta go, but I'll be back."

Her heart thudded with joy. "I'll be waiting."

"Can I do anything for you? Send the boys over to split wood, maybe?"

She shook her head. "It would disqualify me."

Locke grunted. "You always were Irish stubborn." He squeezed her fingers until they tingled then strode out the door.

Valerie followed him to the porch and watched him ride off with Dusty. Just before they rounded a bend, Locke saluted with his Stetson. So did Dusty, who burst into an off-key rendition of a traditional Irish song, "The Girl I Left Behind Me."

Valerie clasped her hands and laughed until tears came. Evidently, Dusty was a lot more observant than she'd suspected!

Chapter Seven

On a late September morning, Valerie surveyed the shining glass jars on the shelves she'd made from scrap lumber off an old, collapsed shed nearby. Sunlight streamed through the windows, targeting the rows of produce harvested from the tiny garden she'd planted. They spelled food for the quickly approaching winter. There was already a chill in the morning air, even though the days remained bright.

Valerie turned to the golden Labrador retriever lying on the braided rag rug next to her cot. Doubt filled her. Was his presence a breach of contest rules? "Of course not," she told the dog. "I didn't ask for you. You simply showed up. If you don't tell, I won't." She managed a small grin. "Even though I suspect Locke had Charley bring you when he delivered flour and sugar and took more of my paintings to town."

Shamrock gave her a doggy smile and thumped his tail on the floor.

Valerie laughed, knelt, and ruffled his fur. Locke rode out as often as he could, but there were still lonely days. Contrary to Charley's prediction, the horde of cowboys he'd claimed would clutter Valerie's doorstep never showed up. Had range gossip gotten around that Locke was calling on her? It would explain her lack of company. She'd wager not many would-be suitors dared brave Locke Stuart's wrath.

Oh, well, Shamrock's a good companion, Valerie decided. She grimaced. Not so the two gimlet-eyed men who came each month to check on her and gave her the third degree. Each time they rode away, she had the feeling they were disappointed to discover she was keeping the spirit as well as the letter of the law laid down in her contract.

So far Whitewind, and particularly Judge Stuart, appeared unaware of Valerie's true identity. She had steadfastly refused to go into town. The less the townsfolk saw of her, the better. She was concerned that some old-timer might recognize her and report to the judge.

"Da always said not to borrow trouble," she told Shamrock. "It has a way of finding you on its own."

Valerie sat back and thought. What would the judge do when he learned that Danny O'Shea's daughter was back? She shuddered. Not for herself, but what it would mean to Locke. "I know You are in control, Lord," she whispered. "Whatever happens, be with us all."

******

Valerie didn't have to wait long for her worst fears to be realized. A few days later Locke rode in looking like a thundercloud.

"Well, the truth is out," he muttered. "Someone put two and two together and decided the artist Valerie Shannon and Shannon O'Shea are one and the same."

She felt sick. "Does your father know?"

"Yes, He also knows I'm in love with you. We had it out, and he's enraged." Locke took her in his arms. "Shannon, will you please give up this scheme of living like a pioneer for a year and marry me?"

Joy exploded inside Janie like a Roman candle. She wanted to scream out, 'Yes. Oh yes. But her common sense snuffed it out.

She gently tried to push him away with a frown, but his arms would not release her. "That would only make things worse."

"I don't see how," he doggedly told her. "Father has already threatened to disinherit me if I ever see you again."

"How can he be so cruel?" Valerie protested, tightening her arms around Locke's waist. "Why should he hate me so?" She leaned her head into his chest. "It's because of Da, isn't it? If only we could prove him innocent of wrongdoing!"

Locke remained silent so long she wondered if he'd heard her. At last he said, "There has to be more to this than what's on the surface. I've tried and tried to discover what it is but so far haven't been able to unearth anything. Unless—"

"—unless the judge knows more about the theft than he's telling," Valerie finished.

"Yes. I've tried not to believe it, but there doesn't seem to be any other logical explanation."

When he finally released her and stepped back, Valerie felt she had never seen such pain in anyone's eyes. She hated to see that look in Locke's eyes.

"Sit down, dear. If we go back over what happened something may stand out."

Locke spread his hands in a hopeless gesture and slumped to a packing box chair. "I've been over it so many times myself, I've lost track."

Valerie knelt on the floor beside him and rested her clasped hands on his knee. "Then once more won't hurt," she soothed.

He stroked her shining hair absentmindedly. "The facts are simple. A valuable necklace went missing. Your father was the only one in the house at the time except Jed and me. Danny denied taking it. So did Jed. And I know that I didn't take it."

"Then, the judge really sent Da to prison on circumstantial evidence only," Valerie murmured bitterly, trying to control her temper.

Locke nodded. "He did."

"Then what happened?"

"Jed rode away a short time later and the necklace was never found?"

"Yes. That's the whole story, at least as far as I ever heard or knew."

Locke stared at her. "I've always wondered if Jed was guilty and for some reason Danny covered for him, hoping my brother would be man enough to own up to what he'd done. That's the kind of man your father was. Besides, he would have known it would break Dad's heart if he ever found out that his favorite son had betrayed him."

Desolation turned Valerie cold. "So, your da lost one son when Jed left, and now he will lose another unless you give me up. Perhaps that would be the best thing you could do."

Locke leaped up. His body turned rigid. His hands became fists. "That won't happen." Face the color of snow, he pulled Valerie to her feet.

"I didn't mean to upset you." Her voice was soft and gentle.

"'Therefore shall a man leave his father and his mother, and shall cleave unto his wife . . .' I will never forsake you, Shannon O'Shea." Determination underlined every word that he spoke.

Valerie knew there would be no changing Locke's mind now that he had chosen his path. Somewhere deep inside a little voice whispered, *You could make the supreme sacrifice and send him away for the sake of his father.*

A heartbeat later, a second voice drowned out the revolting suggestion: *Never! God doesn't expect His servants to be doormats or bow down to tyrants.*

Valerie wrapped her arms around Locke's waist and held him close. Even to return good for the evil she believed Judge Stuart may have wrought she would never let Locke go.

Chapter Eight

September bowed out in a blaze of color. October followed, then November. The calendar on Valerie's wall read December fifth. Surprisingly enough, there had been little snow until today. It had fallen steadily since morning, with no sign of letting up.

"According to Charley, the *Farmer's Almanac* predicts a milder than usual winter," she explained to Shamrock. "I hope so. Even with you for company I don't relish the thought of being snowed in." She chuckled. "Besides, now that the cat's out of the bag and folks know Shannon O'Shea is back, I can go to town as long as the weather holds. Glad my agreement with the *Chicago Tribune* permitted me to have a horse."

"*Woof.*"

"I'll take that as agreement." Valerie stroked the dog's ears. "I've a lot to be thankful for. Dusty was right. My paintings of the scenery around here are bringing in enough money to take care of all of my needs." She felt a blush rise from the frilled collar of her warm dress. "And some left over to start filling my hope chest."

Her spirits sank. The wedding day she had dreamed of for years seemed so distant she sometimes felt depressed. At Valerie's insistence, Locke had offered the judge a compromise.

"Dad roared like a hurricane after I threatened to abandon the Lucky L and elope with you," Locke reported. "He finally agreed to my seeing you as long as there are no immediate plans for a wedding. To be honest, I'm surprised he backed down even that much."

"It's all right," Valerie soothed. "We couldn't have held the wedding until next summer anyway. I need to fulfill my contract with the *Tribune*."

"Why?"

"I gave my word," Valerie answered adamantly. She had come this far and didn't want to fail.

"It's such a long time to wait." Locke sounded dejected, but knew that there was nothing he could do to change the situation.

"Not compared with how long we have already waited for one another," she reminded him.

Locke nodded.

Valerie wanted to assure him that everything between them was fine and in God's hands, but each time he came to see her it was all she could do to keep from crying when he had to leave.

A cheery call interrupted Valerie's musings, followed by the sound of boot heels on the porch. "Ho, the house."

She raced to open the door and noted the white flakes on Locke's Stetson and sheep-lined jacket.

"I didn't think you'd come since it's snowing." She almost pulled him inside.

Locke whacked his hat against his jeans to clear it of snow and shrugged out of his jacket. "Think snow will keep Lariat and me away from our best girl? I admit we can't stay long. It's getting thicker."

"Humph. I had better be your *only* girl," she retorted and peered out at the snow covered ground. She shivered and pulled the door closed.

The teasing light she loved sprang to his blue eyes. "Fishing, aren't you?" Before she could reply he added, "You always were."

"Fishing?"

"My best girl, *mavourneen.*" He dropped a kiss on her forehead, stripped off his gloves, strode across the room and warmed himself at the big wood stove. There was a kettle of soup on top that sent forth a tempting aroma. He glanced around at the decorated room. "You sure have it looking Christmassy in here. I suppose like a true pioneer woman you went into the woods and cut the tree yourself."

"For sure," she boasted. "*And* made the popcorn and cranberry strings. *And* hung the cedar boughs. *And* wrapped the presents." She pointed to the packages under the tree, wrapped in bits of colored dress fabric and tied with bright yarn.

"Presents? Well, I declare, I'd best hie myself to town and see if they have anything fit for my bride-to-be."

Tears brimmed in her eyes. "All I want is you. And to clear Da's name."

Locke's teasing died. "You have the first. I'm still working on the second." He looked as frustrated as Valerie felt.

"I know." An involuntary sigh escaped her. Yet try as hard as she could, she couldn't recapture the light-hearted mood they had shared earlier.

It didn't help when they realized that the snow had thickened and Locke decided that he would leave shortly after they ate.

*****

Valerie watched from the window as Locke rode away. She had no fear of him getting safely home in the snow, but with him gone, her home-for-a-year seemed empty and forlorn.

Disheartened, Valerie washed the few dishes and put them away, then wrapped her arms around Shamrock's neck. Finally able to allow her emotions to flow, tears spilled from her eyes onto his fur.

"Lord, am I foolish for not giving up this crazy life and telling Locke I'll marry him whenever he sets the day?" she prayed.

Her mind flashed over scenes of her life since she had arrived. "I've only been here six months, Lord. How can I stand it for six more? What if Charley and the *Father's Almanac* are wrong?"

Valerie remembered winters here from long ago when the snow had drifted to the roof and no one was able to leave their homes for days on end. It wasn't so bad then, with family, but to face that alone made Valerie shutter.

She recalled how once, when everyone was snowed in, Locke had crawled out of his second-story window and walked on snowshoes across the vast field of snow to get to the O'Shea cottage. It was a good thing he did. The snow had buried the door and trapped them inside. Locke had spent hours shoveling but had finally dug them out.

Valerie hugged her dog. "I wonder if he remembers our O'Shea Christmas traditions." Visions of her father making snow angels with Locke and her brought on a fresh wash of tears. Oddly enough, the sweet memories and hot tears soothed her hurting heart.

"Lord, when he comes to visit again I'll ask him to make snow angels with me, and to read the Christmas story from the Bible and Charles Dickens's *A Christmas Carol.*" These thoughts cheered her some.

Valerie slipped into bed, lulled by the sound of Shamrock's steady breathing and the anticipation of making her childhood traditions live again with Locke. A stanza from a favorite hymn sang in her mind:

Lord, I would place my hand in Thine,
Nor ever murmur nor repine;
Content, whatever lot I see,
Since 'tis my God that leadeth me.

Peace descended like a warm blanket. For better or worse, she was in this place at this time—and never alone. All the snow in the world could not rob her of her Heavenly Father's Presence. She smiled . . . and slept.

Chapter Nine

The snow continued. Valerie and Locke relived years past by making snow angels. Valerie also realized she was not the same person who had left Chicago. Shoveling paths to the lean-to she had built for the horse and to the pump and outhouse had hardened her muscles. She had long since strung ropes between the buildings to prevent losing her way in a snowstorm.

Shortly before Christmas, three feet of glistening white blanketed the ground. Valerie kept a fire going day and night. She thanked God for those who had built the log schoolhouse. No matter how cold it got outside, Valerie and Shamrock remained warm and cozy. She also thanked God for the pump—and kept a kettle of steaming hot water ready to prime it on cold mornings.

One morning Valerie awakened to sapphire skies and intense cold. She ran to the window. The changed world left her speechless. Sparkling icicles hung from tree branches and the porch roof. Sunlight danced on the shimmering snow, painting it red, green, yellow, and blue. Valerie had never seen anything more beautiful.

"This hard freeze means Locke can snowshoe over," she rejoiced. She scurried into warm clothes and fed Shamrock and the horse. She set bread to rise, made stew, and tidied up the room. Then she took down her Bible and curled up on her cot.

Ever since the night when she accepted that she was never alone, she'd relied on the old Book for comfort. It brought a sense of God's nearness.

Valerie turned to where Jesus prayed in the Garden of Gethsemane and slowly read the passage, "'Father, if Thou be willing, remove this cup from Me: nevertheless not My will, but Thine, be done.'"

She closed the Book, feeling she was on the brink of understanding something important. She shut her eyes and reviewed the words. *Not My will, but Thine.* Her thoughts spun.

For months she and Locke had prayed for God to help her clear Da's name. What if they were to follow Jesus' example and leave it in God's hands?

Stunned, she clutched the Bible and whispered, "Is this why You led me here? To learn to wholly rely on You?"

A long-ago plea spoken on a gloomy Chicago day came to mind. *Lord . . . I've worked so hard . . . it isn't enough.*

Trust Me.

The two words brought new understanding. She had stubbornly insisted on clearing her father's name, but neither she nor Locke had done that. Had God been waiting for them to relinquish their pride and trust Him?

"Shannon?"

Was God calling her? "Not unless He's stopping to kick snow off His boots on the porch!" she muttered. The idea made Valerie giggle. She opened the door, gripped Locke's gloved hands, and pulled him inside. Her heart thumped. "I have the most wonderful thing to tell you!" She paused for effect.

Locke smiled. "So . . . what is it?"

Valerie took a deep breath. "You may find this hard to believe, after all I've said about trying to solve the mystery concerning Da. I don't feel that way any longer." She spilled her new revelation. "We need to stop trying to solve the mystery about Da and let God handle it!"

Locke's mouth fell open. Shock and disbelief etched themselves on his face.

Valerie rushed on. "I was reading how Jesus asked God to spare Him before his crucifixion, but then He added, 'not My will, but Thine.' It's what we must do."

Compassion crept into Locke's eyes. He gripped her fingers until they ached. "What if God never proves your father innocent?"

Valerie watched her long-held dream die. Yet the experience she had just gone through sustained her. "So be it. God knows best."

Strong arms encircled her. "I have never been prouder of you or loved you more, my Irish *colleen,*" Locke murmured against her hair.

The sound of stew boiling over onto the hot stove interrupted the tender moment. Yet Valerie knew that if she lived to be older than the Bitterroot Range she would never forget it.

******

On December 23rd, Locke went to bed strangely troubled about his father. For the last week Judge Stuart had little resembled the former self-confident magistrate. Night after night Locke heard him pacing the floor of his study at the Lucky L. He ate little. When questioned, he told Locke to tend to his own affairs and not meddle in things that didn't concern him.

The only clue to the judge's strange behavior was a crumpled, yellow telegram Locke had found in a wastebasket. "Why should the cryptic message, 'it is over' affect Dad so?" Locke asked himself a dozen times. He sighed. "Lord, much as I resented the way he bossed me around, it was better than this. Help me do what Shannon advised: stop trying to solve the mystery and let You handle it."

The next morning dawned clear and cold. Something in his father's face when he came to the breakfast table made Locke stare. The judge looked as if he had fought the hardest battle of his long career.

"I suppose you will be going to see the O'Shea girl today."

Locke felt the hair on the back of his neck rise. "Her name is Shannon."

"Yes." Judge Stuart shook his head when Locke passed a platter of ham and eggs. "Just some coffee."

His aloof manner unnerved Locke. "Something's on your mind, Dad. Spit it out."

"All right." The judge reached into his vest pocket and took out an unsealed envelope. "I want you to take this message to Shannon O'Shea." His lips became a tight seam, then opened enough to say, "I also want your solemn promise you will not open it on the way."

Locke shoved his chair back from the table so hard it overturned. "What's this? More persecution? I thought we agreed—" Suspicion flared, became certainty. "Did you intercept my letters to Shannon? And hers to me?"

The judge's face sagged. "Yes, but that isn't important now."

For the first time in his life Locke wanted to strike his father.

"Not important? All these years I-we thought . . . I'll deliver no message from you, now or ever!" He turned to leave.

His father held out an aged, shaking hand. "Please, Son, this may be the last thing I ever ask of you."

If it hadn't been for the "Please, Son," Locke would have walked away and not looked back. Instead, he took the envelope.

"Do you promise not to read it?" his father asked.

Locke nodded and then he stumbled out the door, desperate to get away from his father but dreading the errand that lay before him.

Chapter Ten

Christmas Eve morning. How different from those of the past! Valerie sang Christmas carols as she waited for Locke to come. Happiness bubbled inside her, the way it had done ever since she turned her quest for justice over to the Lord and promised to accept His will.

"Joy to the world, the Lord is come!"

Shamrock raised his head and added his doggy tenor to her song. But when the door burst open and a white-faced Locke stepped inside, the song died.

"What is it?" Valerie asked, almost afraid to find out why he looked so stricken.

"Father."

Her hand flew to her heart. "Is he hurt?"

"No." Locke's rigid stance didn't relax. "He sent you a message. He made me promise not to read it; said it might be the last thing he would ever ask of me." He reached in his coat pocket and took out a crumpled envelope. "I almost threw it away on the way over, but I had given my word to deliver it, even though I found out he was the one who intercepted our letters."

It was what Valerie had expected, but recriminations wouldn't help. Still, she shrank from touching the envelope. "Read it for me," she implored.

Locke removed the single page. "*Judge Stuart requests Miss O'Shea to accompany him and his son to the Christmas Eve service in Whitewind tonight. It is vitally important.*"

He flung it to the floor. "He has to be up to something. Think I'll let you be the target of some scheme to humiliate you in front of half the town?"

Torn between Locke's suspicion and the invitation, Valerie shook her head. "We have to face it, beloved. Tell your father I shall go." But after Locke left, she rebelled. Why should she give in to the old man's latest whim?

Trust Me.

The words steadied her. Long before Locke returned with a sleigh to take her to the Lucky L, she donned a warm, cherry-red dress over long underwear and several flannel petticoats. Bundled into her hood and long coat, she felt like a mummy.

It didn't take long to reach the ranch. When Judge Stuart joined them in the sleigh, his greeting sent ice worms crawling up and down her spine.

"Thank you for coming, Miss O'Shea."

Valerie nodded, although she longed to confront him and find out why—after all this time—he had acknowledged that Danny O'Shea's daughter still existed.

The drive into Whitewind was silent. When they reached the community church, Locke helped her from the sleigh. He led the way to the Stuart pew and ushered her in. She gave a secret sigh of relief, glad for Locke's protective presence between her and the judge. The church rapidly filled, and the white-haired pastor welcomed the congregation.

"This is a night to relive and recall the coming of our Lord Jesus Christ," he began. "When the angels proclaimed 'peace on earth, good will to men' the shepherds rejoiced. So must we."

"Stop!" Judge Stuart stood and stepped to the aisle.

Heads turned. Silence fell.

Locke looked sick. He reached out a shaking hand to his father. "Dad, not here. Not now. Whatever you have to say can wait."

"No." Some of the judge's former fire echoed throughout the room. "What I have to say has waited too long. Ten years too long."

Locke slumped back in his seat.

Valerie clutched his arm and held her breath. Fortified by God's promises never to leave or forsake her, she waited for what would happen next.

Judge Stuart stepped to the front of the church and faced the congregation. "Ten years ago I sent an innocent man to prison because I honestly believed he had stolen a valuable necklace. Pride blinded me to the possibility one of my sons was guilty." His face twisted. "Even so, I felt sorry for Danny O'Shea's daughter. I kept track of her and –sent anonymous bank drafts until she came of age."

Valerie gasped. So that was where the money had come from!

"Several months ago, a stranger came to me with the truth. My oldest son, in the throes of regret, had confessed he stole the necklace." The judge's shoulders sagged. "Jed said Danny O'Shea knew the truth but offered to take the blame in order to give Jed a second chance."

Tears slipped down Valerie's face.

"Jed failed again and again. He ended up a derelict, ashamed to come home. A single shred of decency caused Jed to want me to know the truth before he died, but the messenger was never to let me know where my son was. Last week I received a telegram telling me it was over. I can only pray that Jed made things right with God before meeting his Master."

A sound like the sighing of a mighty wind moved through the room.

Valerie's heart twisted at the suffering in the judge's face. Locke looked like he had been knifed. But the judge wasn't through. He turned to Valerie.

"Shannon, I should have cleared your father's name when I first discovered the truth. My only defense is that in my grief, I made pride my god. What good would blackening my son's name do? Your father had long since died in prison. True to his character, he was killed while saving the life of a young man being attacked by fellow inmates."

She hadn't known this. How like Da! Sacrificing himself for others. *Greater love hath no man than this, that a man lay down his life for his friends.*

Tears streamed down the judge's lined face. "Ever since the stranger came, I have known no peace. Last night I pleaded with God to forgive me. I believe He has. Shannon, I don't expect you ever can, but I withdraw my opposition to your marrying my son. I will be proud to claim you as a daughter, even if you and Locke cast me away forever." He stumbled down the aisle and out the door.

Strength Valerie didn't know she possessed filled her. "Go after your father," she told Locke. "Bring him back."

Locke wordlessly gripped her hand then marched out. The sound of the door closing behind him sounded loud in the quiet room.

After a moment the pastor quoted, "'I say unto you, that likewise joy shall be in heaven over one sinner that repenteth, more than over ninety and nine just persons, which need no repentance.' Folks, there is no need for a Christmas sermon. We have seen what the power of God can do in a man's life. Let us sing 'Praise God from Whom all Blessings Flow' and never forget this Christmas Eve."

In an agony of suspense, Valerie waited for Locke and his father to return. Suddenly, compassion for the man who had humbled himself before those who had unwisely put Judge Stuart on a pedestal overcame all else. Forgive? Seventy times seven. Not just for the judge's sake. Or Locke's. Or her own. But for the sake of the One Who had led her to an abandoned school house ... and freed her from hatred and the desire for revenge.

Epilogue

For several weeks, winter storms continued to bluster outside the former schoolhouse. None could quench the peace in Valerie's heart. As if to make up for all that had gone before, spring came early. Valerie joyously marked off the days on her calendar. March. April. May. June.

Her long, self-imposed exile was over.

Headlines in the *Chicago Tribune* proclaimed

PIONEER SPIRIT ALIVE AND WELL.

The article went on:

Miss Valerie Shannon O'Shea, who accepted the challenge to live in an abandoned Montana schoolhouse for a full year, has made royally good. She single-handedly fought the elements and walks away with a substantial cash prize. In addition, her Montana landscape paintings are being recognized for their excellence.

However, the biggest prize is Locke Stuart, owner of the Lucky L ranch and Miss O'Shea's childhood sweetheart. They plan to wed on July 4th.

Locke read it and laughed so hard his shoulders shook. "You met their challenge. Now you have another."

Valerie looked at him suspiciously. "What's that?"

He put on an innocent air and drawled, "Taming the Montana cowboy Mr. Stone warned you about."

She crooked her elbows, put her arms on her hips and did an Irish jig. "That, Mr. Locke Stuart, is no challenge. I can twist you around my little finger."

Locke cocked his head and ruefully said, "You already have my father thinking you're the best thing that ever happened to me. I never saw such a change in anyone."

Valerie slid into his arms and rested her head on Locke's chest. Her heart beat in time with his own. Feeling she had at last come home, she silently thanked God.

CHRISTMAS SNOW

by Birdie Etchison

Birdie Etchison was born in San Diego, California, raised in Portland, Oregon and now lives on the Long Beach Peninsula in the SW corner of Washington state. She has had a variety of books published, including juvenile, nonfiction and fiction. She has been included in several anthologies and also writes articles and short stories.

Birdie sold a romance to Woman's World magazine and an article to Grit magazine, both publications she'd tried to sell to for years. Besides teaching at various conferences, she was an instructor for Writer's Digest School for 22 years. Birdie also co-directed Writer's Weekend at the Beach, an annual gathering of writers for 17 years. She served as past president of Oregon Christian Writers, and is still active in that organization. In 2013, she was included in a book: *Legendary Locals of the Long Beach Peninsula.* Sydney Stevens, author.

Chapter One

I hate snow, Janie Montgomery thought as a truck zoomed by, throwing more of the slushy, wet snow on Janie's windshield. Blinded, she clutched the wheel as the car slid into a ditch. She sat, shaking, wondering how that happened. Would she ever make it to Spokane? Why had she said yes to her aunt's request to come for Christmas?

"Snow is not predicted," Aunt Lou had said.

Not so. Not expected, yet here it was. It hit the windshield and Janie marveled at the fat flakes. She had to find something positive in this situation. She wondered what to do next when a sudden tap on the window made her jump.

A tall, slender man in a long, heavy coat and a stocking cap pulled down over his ears, stood peering in.

Janie rolled the window down, but said nothing. Words couldn't escape the tight knot in her throat.

"I can pull your Camry out," he said.

"Will it be drivable?" she finally asked. She didn't know what she'd do without her car. How could she get to Aunt Lou's?

His smile grew wider. "I'm thinking it will. Put it in neutral after I hook you up."

The wind blew her hair and she shivered. She needed a hat. Any kind of hat would do. She hoped Aunt Lou had extra hats and gloves. Knowing her aunt who saved everything, she figured she would.

The Good Samaritan brought a chain, which he hooked to her front bumper. He bent down and she felt as if he were an angel coming along when he did. She didn't even know his name.

"Okay!" He held up his arm. "Put it in neutral and you'll be out in no time."

She closed her eyes, praying it would work. The car shifted and then with one big pull, it was on the road again.

He came back and said he'd look under the car for damage.

"Are you a mechanic?" she asked, climbing out of the car.

"Not really. I'm an EMT and it's my day off. I knew I'd find someone in trouble out here in this first snowstorm of the year."

The flakes hit her face as she looked around. Snow was beautiful. Magical, somehow. If one didn't have to drive in it.

Five minutes later she stood holding the man's business card and watched him sprint back to his SUV and get in. "If you need anything, just call me," he'd said.

Greg Kinkaid. There were two numbers. Why would he give her his card? Did he figure she'd be in a ditch again before arriving at her destination?

She sat on the side of the road, trying to get the courage to forge ahead. Greg said Spokane was twenty miles away. He also told her to follow tracks on the road, or get behind a slow moving vehicle as she drove east.

*****

She thought back to the call from Aunt Lou. Her real name was Louise, but Janie had never called her anything but Aunt Lou. She was her mother's older sister. She swallowed hard, remembering back to the day before her mother died. Christmas was only ten days away.

The decorated house was on the walking tour in the small suburban Seattle town. Her mother decorated anything that stood still. The bathroom had snowflake toilet tissue; snowmen filled every corner of the house. The mammoth tree reached the ceiling and could be seen from the street. Garlands, twinkling lights, a manger scene on the hearth. Huge red felt stockings hung from the mantel.

Janie's mother loved doing it. Her special Christmas tea brewed on the stove and a plate of sugar cookies cut in holiday shapes sat on the sideboard for guests to taste. It was Janie's favorite time of year.

Then it suddenly ended.

One night they were returning from the discount store with one more string of lights. "We're also going to decorate the hall this year," her mother said, as if she had to explain.

"Janie, your turn to sit in back." Her mother had held the door open. "Susie wants to ride up front with me."

Snuggled in the back seat, with wonderful thoughts of decorations and cookies in her mind, she never saw the car coming. All she remembered were her mother's scream and sister's frenzied shouts that filled the air.

Two days later Janie was told that her mother and sister died instantly in the crash. She had been rushed to the hospital.

Janie lived, but the memories of what she'd lost made her wish she'd died, too. Aunt Lou arrived that day, holding Janie's hand, murmuring over and over how much she loved her and that Janie would come to live at her house.

"No!" Janie'd cried. She couldn't bear the thought to leave the only home she'd ever known.

Aunt Lou moved in a week later, staying until Janie turned eighteen.

The snow now fell faster and Janie's heart felt heavy, so very heavy. She would miss her apartment, and what if David came around? She was certain he would not – said he had to break it off and left without waiting for her response. She guessed she hadn't known David after all. Maybe she wasn't supposed to get married.

*****

Greg Kinkaid turned off the freeway and headed toward his brother's house. The thought of that young woman stayed with him. Her crooked smile and the way her deep blue eyes watched him, as if she thought he might do something wrong.

He turned on the disk player and put Elvis Presley's Christmas CD in. He loved Christmas music. Three weeks until the holidays and he had no one with whom to share the joy with. There was a brother and sister-in-law, but not a girlfriend.

Please have snow
And mistletoe
And presents under the tree

Greg thought of the young woman again, wishing he'd asked her name. She knew his. Would she call him? Probably not. Unless she got into trouble and he didn't want that to happen.

I hear the bells saying Christmas is here
Why can't every day be like Christmas?

Greg tugged on his beard – he'd only started growing it after his thirtieth birthday. Why? He didn't know. Maybe it was because someone said he had a baby face. What guy wants a young looking face?

He pulled up in front of his brother's house. He parked, hurried up the steps and threw the door open. Annabelle must have dinner in the oven. The whole house smelled wonderful.

"Hey, am I staying for dinner?"

She turned and smiled. "As if you need to ask."

"Where are the decorations?" he asked, pouring a cup of coffee from the pot on the counter.

"Don't know if we're going to do them this year."

"Not decorate?" He stared at Annabelle, and then knew why. She was seven months pregnant and so far had experienced a rough pregnancy. Decorating was the last item on her agenda.

"So, what are you doing out on your day off?" She asked.

Greg shrugged. "Just out looking for possible accidents. You know how it is when the first snow hits."
Annabelle placed a pan of cornbread next to the casserole she had in the oven. "When are you going to settle down, Greg? Find a nice woman and get married?"

Greg pulled a chair out. "Back to that, are you Annabelle?"

"You're the older brother. In Bible times, the oldest brother had to marry first." She gave her brother a sly smile.

"Yeah, well." He got up and stretched. Time to change the subject. "I'll decorate your house if you tell me where everything is."

"You'd do that?"

"Why not? If you feed me, I suppose it's the least I can do."

"Let's see what Rich thinks."

"He's too busy. Isn't he painting the nursery this weekend?"

Annabelle placed a hand on her rounded middle. "Yes, he promised he would."

"I'd rather decorate than paint. How about if I come by on Saturday?"

The bell rang on the oven. Annabelle turned it off. "Wonder where Rich is?"

"He'll be here. He can probably smell dinner at work."

Annabelle sat down and put her feet up. "Gotta take a load off. This young one can certainly kick. Don't know if I can wait another two months."

"I Don't think you're the one to decide," Greg chuckled.

*****

Janie kept driving behind slow vehicles, but each time they'd begin to go faster than she wanted to.

Why didn't this snow stop? It had piled high on both sides of the road. She glanced at her cell phone to see if anyone had called. Looking away for that length of time caused her car to begin to slide.

She slammed the brakes. Mistake number two. The car swayed back and forth. Holding her breath she prayed the car would stop. It had to stop. Out of her control, the car slid across the road and into another ditch. Now her car faced in the wrong direction and she couldn't get it to move.

Janie began to cry.

*****

Greg brought his sister-in-law a glass of water and told her to stay tight. He'd set the table, or do whatever she needed done.

His sister stared at him as if he were a stranger. Greg was a nice guy, but didn't usually offer to do domestic chores for her.

"Why are you fidgeting?" Annabelle asked. "You seem nervous about something."

Greg got up and refilled his coffee cup. He knew it was silly to think about that girl on the highway, but he couldn't shake the memory of her face.

Is that why I feel the need to keep moving tonight? What was it about her that is making me feel this way? I'm a bundle of nerves.

Annabelle grinned. "Can't wait to see what you do once the baby is here. I'll bet you'll be a great uncle."

Greg nodded. "Maybe. If it's a boy, I'll take him out on calls with me," he teased.

Annabelle shook her head. "Not until he is a lot older."

Greg laughed. "I still don't know why you guys don't want to know the baby's sex. Now you have to paint the nursery yellow."

"It's just the way we feel about things." The clock on the mantle chimed. A worried look crossed Annabelle's face. "I Sure hope Rich hasn't been in an accident somewhere."

Greg walked over and patted her hand to soothe her. "I'm sure he is fine.

Just then Greg's cell phone rang. He knew it would be someone stranded on the road. It never ceased to amaze him how many people didn't know the concept of slow down when it snowed.

"Guess I'll take a rain check on the dinner, or maybe I should say *snow* check."

Not waiting for Annabelle's comment, he hurried out the door and down the sidewalk covered with a blanket of snow. So much for a day off.

Chapter Two

Janie looked at the card that was grasped in her hand. She didn't call the number immediately. How could she admit to being so stupid? Only she could do something like slide into a ditch twice. This time she could have been hit by oncoming traffic, but everyone was going slowly.

Just then a woman pulled alongside the car. "Should I call 911?"

Janie shook her head. "No, but thanks. I'm calling a friend."

A friend? Where did that come from? She didn't even know him. It would have been simpler and possibly quicker if she'd called 911. But he had answered and said he would be right there. She didn't mention who she was; he didn't give her a chance. Maybe he knew, already.

Janie got out of the car, away from the traffic. She pulled her jacket closer. Another person stopped and she repeated that help was coming. People were certainly nice here. Thoughtful. Helpful. Maybe it was the season.

Janie thought about Aunt Lou again. Perhaps she should call her to say she was on her way. Knowing her aunt she probably thought Janie got a late start. It was a five-hour trip.

A car honked and she looked away. The Camry was in a precarious position and something told her there would be damage this time. How could she have glanced away for even half a minute?

Another honk sounded; two short beeps, the kind someone does when they know you. She looked at the car behind her and nodded. What could she possibly say?

"I had a feeling it was you," Greg said as he walked up, carrying a blanket. "I'm calling a tow truck – I can't get you out of this." He looked down at her. "Are you all right?"

She shivered and he threw the blanket around her shoulders. "Let's go wait in my car. After the tow truck comes, I'll give you a ride home. Think you said you were going to Spokane. Is someone waiting for you?"

Janie nodded. "My aunt. She lives in Veradale – it's out of Spokane a ways." She looked away. His bold gaze made her tremble.

"I've been an EMT for eight years and this is the first time I helped the same person twice in one day."

Janie chewed her upper lip.

"I don't mind – just so you know."

"You said it was your day off." Janie glanced at him sideways. "I promise I won't bother you again."

"You're not going to be able to drive that car. In fact, you may need to get a new one."

Janie smiled. "I'll drive Aunt Lou's. Guess that solves that problem."

"Good thinking."

"I can't abandon my car," Janie said. "Even if it isn't drivable, there's stuff to get out."

Greg nodded. "Of course. I'll get it."

Jane stared at his large arms, knowing he could carry twice as much as she could and was thankful for his kind gesture.

"I need to help."

"You're cold. You're not dressed properly for this kind of weather."

Greg took her hand. They crept across the road to the SUV. She felt comfort, knowing the pavement was slippery. Her black flats were the worst things to wear in snow. That's all she needed - to be without her car and laid up with a sprained ankle. She got to the SUV and Greg held the passenger door open.

"Stay here. I'll put your stuff in the back. Just cleaned it out; have lots of room. Three trips should do it."

 He looked back and Janie wondered how she could have met someone so nice. Handsome, too.

Greg brought the two boxes of Christmas decorations from the car. "Hey, you have a lot of Christmas stuff. What are you going to do with this?"

Janie thought of the homemade place mats her mother had made years ago. And the crèche. They always brought a lump to her throat.

"Going to decorate Aunt Lou's house."

He stacked the boxes on the floor. "I – " his eyes met her gaze. "Have an idea."

Was he going to help her with this, too?

"What might that be?"

"I'll tell you when I finish getting your things," he said and made his way back out the door.

Two more trips and he'd brought everything from the car, even the small box of tools. She'd never used any of them, but she was prepared since a friend told her she needed the basics.

The truck arrived and Greg handed the driver the keys to her car. "Let's go. The towing company will take your car to the nearest town. It's not far from your aunt's."

"You don't have to take me to Aunt Lou's. I could call a taxi."

He turned, his bushy eyebrows arched. "You can't mean that. Taxi's cost." He closed one eye. "About forty dollars. I can think of a lot of places that could use forty bucks if you just want to get rid of money."

Janie stared for a moment and then broke into a laugh. "As far as that goes, I can think of places to use it, too."

He climbed in and put the vehicle in gear. "Here's the thing, Janie. I will help you with hanging the lights and doing anything that is high and out of reach for you. But…"

She had started to sputter.

"Wait until I'm through. In return, you can help me decorate my brother's tree. He's far too busy and his wife is expecting and having a few problems."

"Oh, nothing serious, I hope."

"I do hope not."

"I think that's a great idea. And I'm going to bake the cookies my mother always made."
"Made? You mean like homemade?"

"Yes." Janie only hoped she could make them taste as good. She had to tell Greg about her mom and sister. Might as well get it over with.

"My mom died, you know."

His dark eyes widened. "Died?"

"And my little sister. Six years ago."

Janie felt her heart dive, as it always did when thinking about her loss – especially this time of year.

"Wow. That's terrible."

"That's why I'm going to Aunt Lou's. I have no family left in Seattle." She certainly didn't need to tell him about David. The less said, the better.

The snow grew heavier and the windshield wipers adjusted to get rid of it. A second later, Christmas music filled the car.

"I can't believe the snow is coming down so hard. Looks like a white Christmas to me," Greg said.

Ten minutes later, Greg pulled up in front of a coffee house. "The weather may get worse, but I've got to have coffee. It's dinnertime, too, you know."

Janie nodded. Darkness fell and she glanced at her watch. Six o'clock. No wonder it was dark

"I need to call Aunt Lou to tell her I'm coming a bit later than I thought."

"No need to mention the accident," he said.

"No, I won't."

Greg sprinted around the SUV and opened the passenger door. Janie still had the blanket around her. "Maybe I should stay here." She eyes the snow-covered sidewalk. You could bring coffee to me."

"No. I have a better idea."

In less than a minute, he had taken a flat looking shovel out of the back and shoveled the sidewalk leading up to the coffee house. He returned to the car with a look of triumphant pride. "There. How's that look?"

It had to be because he was an EMT. He probably could do anything. Like take her blood pressure. She didn't want him to do that now, as she was sure it had risen to an unbelievable number just watching his muscles while he worked.

"We need sandwiches, too. This is a good place."

Janie thought of her wallet. She had less than five dollars left and didn't want to say anything.

"It's my treat. It's not every day I get to rescue a woman twice. The least I can do is pay for coffee and a bite to eat."

Janie liked the feel of his arm on her, guiding her up the sidewalk. Would David have done this? She doubted it.
Three days ago her world had seemed pointless, though she tried to remember that God was taking care, watching out for her. Going to Aunt Lou's was a good idea. She had Christmas time off since her boss laid people off in December and January and she had been one of them.

Greg removed his hat and gloves when they entered the coffee shop. She was secretly glad to see no sign of a wedding band, however, with his job as EMT, he might not wear one. It could be dangerous for him to wear on the job, or so she'd heard.

"What do you think of my plan?"

Janie smiled as they stood in line. "You mean the decorating?"

"Yes."
"I think Aunt Lou would be pleased."

"Rich and Annabelle will be, too."

Janie ordered a toasted cheese and a cup of plain black coffee. Greg ordered a sandwich, plus two cookies for dessert. He chose mocha.

"Find us a table and I'll bring the order."

There was one left in a corner and Janie hurried over. Janie, usually shy, found it difficult to talk to men a lot of times, but she talked to Greg as if they'd been friends forever.
She still couldn't believe any of this was happening. Soon she'd be at Aunt Lou's. Once the two houses were decorated, that would be it. Yet a tiny shred of hope coursed through her veins. Maybe that wouldn't be it. Maybe they could be friends and take in a movie sometime. Or she could fix her favorite meal that she cooked for guests. Pot roast. With onions, potatoes, carrots, smothered in thick roast gravy.

By the time they'd finished the food and drink, the snow had stopped. As Janie went out, she stopped and marveled at the sight.

"We have so little snow in Seattle, and when it comes, it almost always becomes a mess of dirty slush before long."

"So I've heard. Do you like living there?"

Janie shrugged. "Guess I'll find out during the next few weeks."

He patted her shoulder. "I'm guessing you'll like it here. Lived here all my life. Know most everyone. Heard about your aunt, but not met her."

"Hey, that's probably good," Janie said. "That means she's had no falls or heart attacks."

"Yep. You're right there."

"Does your mother like to decorate?" Janie asked.

The car swerved to the right. Greg stared straight ahead.

"She used to."

Janie bit her lip as she realized she had touched on a painful spot.

"Oh, has she passed, too?"

He still didn't look at her, but his voice dropped low. "She's in a care facility."

"I'm sorry to hear that." Janie wished she'd never brought it up.

"She doesn't know us now. She's lost her memory. It's some form of dementia."

Janie took a deep breath. *His mother must be too ill for family members to care for. Everyone has a heartache of some sort.*

"I'm sorry I asked," she finally said.

"No." His voice sounded flat. "Don't be. I need to talk about it more. Need to try to understand. It's just so hard."

"Maybe we can go decorate her room," Janie said.

A questioning look crossed his face as he turned in her direction. "Don't think so, but I'll ask about it."

Janie smiled and started singing along with *Jingle Bells.*

"What's the address?" Greg asked then.

Janie fumbled in her purse, but there was no envelope there. She'd written it on the back of one, the first thing she found next to the telephone. She'd been here a few times, but had never come alone.

"I think I lost it, but don't know how."

"What's her telephone number?

Janie dug her cell phone out of her pocket and sighed as she saw the *Battery low* sign.

"Give me her last name. I can look it up in a second on my I-phone." Greg pulled off the road and put the car in neutral.

"Don't like to talk or look up anything while driving. Especially in this weather."

Seconds later he'd found it. "We're about a mile away! Good thing."

Janie felt a tingle of excitement at the thought of seeing her aunt again. She added this to her keyed up state from meeting and spending time with Greg. It all seemed so natural. God had sent him to help out and he'd done more than any one could ever expect.

When they reached her aunt's house, Greg pulled up in front and turned off the motor.

"Here you go." He nodded towards the house.

Janie slipped open the car door, but then turned back, concern flashed on her face. "You have to meet Aunt Lou."

"I will." His eyes promised, so Janie turned toward the house. "Go on in and I'll grab the decorations and your bags and bring them."

The porch light shone in the darkness. Janie held onto the railing, not sure if the steps were slippery or not.

"Wait." Greg said. He ran to the back of the vehicle and got the shovel again. In no time her aunt's sidewalk and steps were clear of snow. Greg quickly bounced two bags on the porch before Janie even got to the door.

Aunt Lou must have heard their voices or the thumps on the porch, because before Janie could even knock she opened the door and stepped out.

"Janie, you're here. Finally!" She shielded her eye when Greg sprinted up the steps with the next load. "And this is a friend? Not David."

Janie's face colored, hoping Greg had not heard. If he had, he did not let on.

"No, Auntie. This is Greg, the EMT who rescued me more than once. My car is totaled; sorry about that."

"You're okay? Not hurt?" Her aunt hugged her close.

"No, thank heavens."

"I was just getting ready to make hot chocolate."

"Sounds great," Greg's voice boomed out enthusiastically. "This is the last load. Now to get it into the house."

Minutes later they ate gingersnaps and hot chocolate with mounds of whipped cream.

Lou was a talker, as was Greg. Janie had to laugh to herself. She could just sit here and listen to the two of them chat.

"We're going to decorate your house on my next day off," Greg promised. "Hope that's okay."

"Marvelous!" Lou clapped her hands. "I usually get my neighbor to bring a tree in and put the star on the top, then I decorate it, but I haven't hung lights for years."

"We're going to do all of that," Janie added. "And then I'll help Greg decorate his brother's house."

"It's about fifteen miles away," Greg explained. "You've heard of the Hamilton Heights area?"

Lou's smile froze. "Had a very good friend once who lived over that way."

Janie wondered who that friend might have been. She would ask later.

Soon they chatted away again. Janie stifled a yawn, thinking how long the day had been.

"Say, thanks for the cookies and hot chocolate," Greg said. "I need to get back. Have to work in the morning."

"Can't thank you enough." Janie smiled up at him. She caught her breath when he smiled.

"Glad I had the day off and got to meet both of you."

Janie walked him to the door. Greg turned and took her hand for a brief moment. "I'll be in touch. Need to touch base on all three decorating plans."

Chapter Three

Janie couldn't sleep. She turned the bed-side lamp on and reached for a book. She never went to bed without taking two books with her. One a mystery, the other a romance. It depended on her mood which one she read.

She was used to the bed; this was the room she'd slept in since she could remember. A four-poster bed was romantic. The flowered quilt, the matching daisy curtains, the pale yellow walls.

What made her not sleepy? The day had been gruesome. How could she have gone in the ditch twice? She recalled the look on her aunt's face when she explained what happened. Aunt Lou hadn't -believed it.

"The conditions were just right," Greg had said. "I've seen it happen with experienced drivers. Happens in a flash."

Janie had watched Greg as he talked. She admired him. Liked his attitude. His smile made her tingle.

"Stop it," she suddenly said aloud bringing an end to the thoughts. "He is a rescuer; does it every day. Probably has helped hundreds of women out of ditches over the winter months."

Janie punched her pillow, turned the light off and snuggled under the quilt, glad she'd brought her fleece pajamas.

The TV in the other room was still on; Aunt Lou never retired until midnight. Janie remembered her mother remarking on it. "I was the early riser, but Lou slept in because she'd been up half the night. I remember her making a lemon meringue pie at three a.m. one time."

Her mother had told her that Aunt Lou'd had a brief "fling" once as she called it, but Aunt Lou insisted that it wouldn't have worked out.

"How can a morning person marry a night person?" She had stated.

"You could have compromised," Janie's mother had told her. "It happens all the time."

Janie shook her head. She knew now why Aunt Lou had reacted so strongly to Greg's mention of Hamilton Heights. It must have been where her boyfriend had been from.

Janie decided that she wouldn't bring it up; no sense in making auntie feel bad.

Now as Janie lay in bed, no closer to sleep than before, the day continued to flash through her mind like a movie.

A sudden tap sounded on her door. She bolted up. Aunt Lou? How did she know Janie was still awake?

"I'm awake," she called out, springing from the bed and opening the door. "Let's have a pajama party."

Aunt Lou chuckled. "Just remembered the cookie jar is empty and thought I might bake some chocolate chip dreams."

"Oh, Aunt Lou, those are to die for. I could help, if you like."

"I had a feeling that you weren't sleeping. And I think I know why."

Janie felt her cheeks color. Her aunt always had been intuitive. She'd come to Seattle last Thanksgiving and met David. Janie had refused her Aunt's advice then.

"So what do you think of David?" Janie had asked, clasping her hands hopefully. Aunt Lou's opinion meant a lot to her.

"He's very nice, Janie, but don't think he's your type."

"My type? What is my type?" Janie had asked disappointingly.

"Footloose and fancy free. And David just doesn't fit that mold."

Janie remembered laughing. Aunt Lou had these crazy sayings – some Janie had not heard before. "Maybe I can teach him how?"

Lou shook her head. "Don't get the idea that you can change a person. It just doesn't work out."

Her aunt had said no more, and Janie had laughed it off at the time, but now that what her aunt had said had become a reality, Janie realized that her Aunt may have more insight than she did. At least she planned on listening more carefully to her aunt in the future.

Janie grabbed her robe and scooted her feet into her fuzzy slippers. These items stayed here at Aunt Lou's all year round for Janie's visits.

*****

Greg returned to his apartment, unable to concentrate. He paced the floor – something he rarely did. With his job, he kept busy enough that pacing wasn't part of the routine.

What had happened today that made him feel so different? He had dated so many girls. Some Annabelle had invited over for dinner. Others he knew from work, but he had never reacted this way.

Shelley was an EMT and every–one thought they were made for each other. And they were, so it seemed. He'd even gotten so far as to look at rings. Then she had up and moved. He never found out why. She didn't answer his calls.

He sighed. That was more than five years ago and he was over the relationship, but it left him gun shy, as his brother put it. Not wanting to try again. However, Janie had stirred something inside him.

Janie didn't wear a ring. He'd noticed, especially since she didn't wear gloves. She had a way about her he liked. Kind of laid back. Yet he knew she had goals and was not self-centered as Shelley had been. There had been mention of a David, but he'd pretended not to hear. Of course, he did wonder who David was.

Greg ran his hand through his hair. He grabbed the remote, put one of the late night talk shows on, determined to forget about the day, but his mind kept wandering so he turned it off. The daily newspaper didn't help either. He looked around his apartment and knew he had to decorate and soon. That would put him in a good mood.

His beeper went off. He jumped up. An accident – over on Illinois Avenue – two cars involved. Greg reached for his jacket and gloves and headed out. Obviously, he wasn't meant to sleep.

As he raced to the scene, his mind kept seeing Janie and that look of shock and then amusement when he helped her the first time. He thought about her when he was watching Annabelle prepare dinner. When he noticed Annabelle's swollen legs, he wondered what Janie would look like if she were with child?

Where had that thought come from? For goodness sake, he'd just met the woman.

The Medics beat Greg to the accident scene. He parked and rushed over to administer first aid. It wasn't necessary. Two people had died – probably instantly. The truck's hood was smashed, and the driver paced back and forth.

"I need to check your pulse." Greg tried to get the man to sit.

"No need." The man shook his head. "They turned right in front of me. I tried but couldn't stop. You gotta believe me."

"I do believe you. Now calm down. Let me check a few things. You should go to the hospital for a check-up."

"What about the others? Why aren't you helping them?"

"Waiting for the coroner," Greg murmured, hating to be the bearer of bad news.

"No!" The man threw his cap on the ground. "I had no idea – no idea."

The man sank to his knees and Greg was able to take his pulse. He continued to speak softly, trying to calm the man.

After the bodies were removed and the man was on his way to the hospital as a precaution, Greg was able to return home.

As he walked back to his car, Greg shook his head. Two young women dead. A tragedy. They had been drinking, a lot; he'd smelled the alcohol immediately. He got back in his SUV and turned east. He didn't realize what he was doing until he saw the Veradale sign.

He drove by Lou's house and stopped in front. He could see lights blazing in the kitchen. *Was something wrong? Who would be up at this hour?* He checked the time. Two a.m.!

He could see two forms through the curtained window. *What were they doing?*

Greg knew it was ridiculous, but he found himself parking, walking up the sidewalk he'd shoveled earlier. Waited a minute and rang the bell.

*****

Lou peeked through the peephole, a bit curious a bit concerned, wondering who could be at the door this late, or rather this early in the morning. When she saw Greg she swung the door open.

"Mr. Kinkaid! What are you doing here?"

She turned and hollered, "Take that first batch out, Janie. We have a guest."

Janie froze on the spot. *Greg had come back? Why on earth was he in this part of town?* He'd told her where he lived and it was a good twelve miles away.

Janie looked down and realized she was in her robe and slippers-, but there was nothing she could do about it now.

She grabbed a potholder and opened the oven door. The cookies were perfect. She removed the sheet and put in the second one. Aunt Lou never cooked two sheets at a time.

"They don't cook evenly," was her reasoning.

Footsteps sounded down the hall. Aunt Lou entered the kitchen first.

"Oh, perfect! You got them out at the precise right moment."

Greg shook his head. He looked at Janie and smiled. "Had a call nearby. Decided to drive over this way." He grinned. "Expected to see a dark house buttoned up for the night. When I saw the light on, I decided to stop and check if everything was okay."

"Well, sit down and have some cookies and milk. I take it you like milk?" Lou teased.

Greg pulled out a chair, wondering if Janie was going to talk. She looked as if she were in shock. It made him think of the man in the truck. He should check to see if he'd been discharged.

"I love chocolate," Greg said, reaching for a still warm cookie.

"Aunt Lou puts mint chips in hers. They are special," Janie finally spoke.

"And a glass for you?" Aunt Lou said, glancing at Janie. She already had three glasses, three small plates and the milk.

Janie nodded. "Maybe it will help me sleep." She turned and explained. "I was having trouble sleeping, so Aunt Lou offered to let me share in her late night cookie baking."

Greg reached for another cookie. He took a bite. "Mmm. Best I've ever had. Entered any cooking contests, Lou?"

Aunt Lou laughed as she sat. "Actually, I did a couple of times. Got blue ribbons at the State Fair."

"That was for a cake she makes that is mighty tasty and so different."

Greg grinned. "So you had trouble sleeping?" He looked at Janie. "Sometimes it's hard to sleep after an accident."

"Too much going on," Lou answered. "It's not every day Janie drives her car into a ditch."

"I didn't drive into the ditch," Janie sputtered.

"She didn't drive into it; that's the problem," Greg joked. "She just nonchalantly let it happen."

Janie rolled her eyes. "Whatever."

"I think I'd best be on my way." Greg stood and pushed his chair under the table. "Can't believe I'm eating cookies with two women at this hour."

Janie stood. "When are we decorating?"

"So you remembered." He ambled toward the door. "My next day off is Thursday. I think we can get this house and my brother's place decorated."

"And the home?"

"We can do that on Saturday – I'm off early."

Lou handed Greg a small bag of cookies. "For you to enjoy tomorrow."

Greg let himself out, wanting to look back, but not daring. He knew he would remember Janie's flushed cheeks, the smile that crept across her face, the way she broke the cookie in half. He'd gobbled his in two bites. He grabbed one from the bag and ate it before turning toward home.

*****

"Well now," Lou said as she locked the front door. "Wasn't that a nice surprise?"

Janie remained silent.

"Not going to say anything?"

What was there to say? First, she needed to stop her pounding heart. But she didn't think that would happen for a while. This man had entered her life and seeing him three times in one day and having food with him and cookies tonight. At three A.M. was just too bizarre.

"Janie, I am good at judging character, as you already know."

Janie's head flew up, her eyes full of dread. "Yes, Auntie, you are."

"Some men flirt and you need to take that into consideration. Not get your hopes up and be disappointed."

Janie's shoulders dropped. "As if I don't know that." She assumed she was reading too much into Greg's kind and gentle behavior. But her aunt knew best.

Aunt Lou stomped her foot lightly. "I wasn't finished with my spiel. Don't jump to conclusions. Let me finish." It was one thing about Aunt Lou. She could talk an auctioneer down, given the chance.

Janie stared sorrowfully at the woman. She hated to hear the words that would confirm that Greg was no better for her than David had been.

"Go ahead."

"Greg is a wonderful young man and I can tell he likes you very much." Aunt Lou's words surprised her, but she hesitated. Reality had finally taken the place of her beating heart.

"He's thirty."

"So, that makes him six years older than you – that doesn't matter."

"Aunt Lou, stop. Even if Greg is wonderful, and even if he likes me, I can't stay in Spokane. My home and job are in Seattle."

"You can get a job here."

"I like Seattle."

"Home is where the heart is."

Janie sighed. Another saying. It wouldn't matter what her argument might be, Aunt Lou would make it seem meaningless.

"He has a girlfriend."

Lou raised an eyebrow. "You know that for a fact?"

Janie couldn't lie. Every one knew if she lied. "I think so."

"As I thought." Lou took another cookie. "I believe he's lonely. I also believe he is looking for someone, though he may not know it yet."

"I don't think so."

"Christmas is the season for caring. Sharing. For love if you're in the market for that sort of thing."

Janie stared out the window at the crisp cold sky. "David might come back." Her voice was soft but the words sounded unconvincing.

"And the neighbor's rooster won't crow in the morning," her aunt's voice was sharp.

Janie sighed. She wasn't able to think about this now. She was finally feeling tired.

"It's late, Auntie. Shouldn't we go to bed?"

"I suppose. You go on ahead while I put the cookies away and clean up the kitchen."

"It can wait. I'll do it in the morning."

"I'm not sleepy," Lou gave Janie a hug.

Janie wanted to say that she wasn't tired either, but she said nothing. She just walked down the hall toward the bedroom.

After a moment, she shook her head and crawled back into bed for the second time that night, but once again her mind continued to replay the evening.

Stop, she admonished herself. *Greg is a kind man. He may even be a bit lonely. But…* Janie grinned. She knew that if given a day, Aunt Lou would find out everything there was to know about him. It was just her way.

Janie's heart had never reacted to anyone like it had tonight and earlier. She knew that she needed to get it together. She wasn't some young starry-eyed girl.

Janie kept reminding herself, *Friends. That's all. She and Greg were simply friends.*

Chapter Four

Greg called, saying he was on his way over. "My day off."

Aunt Lou hopped from the kitchen to the living room. Janie had never seen her so excited. "It'll be like the Christmases your mom and I had as young girls."

She paused in the doorway to the kitchen. "I'm making buttermilk pancakes. I do hope Greg hasn't eaten a big breakfast."

"He is a guy, you know, Auntie."

"Yes." She grinned. "And if he's like most guys I know, they can eat again an hour later. I've never been able to put away food like a man."

Janie opened the boxes – the Christmas tree ornaments were on the large coffee table. Two chairs had been removed to make room for the huge Noble fir.

"I ordered it online," Aunt Lou explained. "It was pretty expensive, but at Christmas who cares?"

"It will be the loveliest ever," Janie exclaimed.

"When is Greg coming? I'll wait to start the pancakes."

"He said he was on his way. Maybe he found another woman in a ditch."

"Now there's a bit of humor," Lou laughed.

As if on cue, the SUV pulled up just then. Janie ran to the door and opened it.

Greg had come with two ladders, a step and one to use to get on the roof.

Janie's eyes lit up. "Did you have breakfast?"

He set the ladders down and smiled at Janie. "A piece of toast and a banana."

Janie smiled. "Aunt Lou has something more filling than that for you."

Six pancakes, four strips of bacon and a dish of home canned pears later, Greg finally made his way out of the kitchen and started on the tree. Janie couldn't believe he'd eaten so much. Auntie was right, as usual.

Once the tree was firmly in the tree stand, Lou covered the base with a bright red skirt. The lights came next – five full strings. Then Auntie started putting bulbs on.

Four hours later, the lights flashed on and the decorations all glittered brightly. It was beautiful. The crèche was on a table since Lou didn't have a fireplace and it also looked wonderful.

Greg had also put lights along the outside eaves and had placed a huge star on the roof.

Standing back and admiring the house with Janie and Lou, Greg explained. "The star is what it's all about. You know, the true meaning of Christmas. People tend to forget that."

"Amen," Janie added.

"No Santas for us. And no snow this morning. I'm thankful for that." He moved toward the house and plugged in the lights.

"Just wish it was dark; it would show up better, but it will look really nice tonight."

Lou clasped her hands with pleasure. "I can't thank you enough, young man."

"No problem. I think your breakfast was thanks enough. You cook like that and I'll come help you anytime."

Janie loved the way that Greg spoke to Aunt Lou. He seemed to genuinely care for her. That was something that David had not been able to do.

Janie shook off the thought. "It's time to go to Greg's brother's house." She didn't add that she looked forward to meeting his family. She hoped that she could be as friendly to them as Greg had been to Aunt Lou.

"Their house is smaller," Greg explained. "Won't take us as long. And we'll have something to eat there as well.

Annabelle loves to cook, just like your aunt."

Janie sighed. "Cooking is a dying art."

"I agree. Most of my married friends get served microwave meals for dinner. I personally love a home cooked meal, dessert and all."

"Oh, that reminds me. I forgot to mention we'd like you to help decorate cookies next week, if that's possible," Janie said. She felt comfortable talking to Greg. It was as if they'd known each other forever.

"That sounds good. Decorating, you say?"

"Yeah. Sugar cookies. We'll take a big plateful to church the Sunday before Christmas."

"Maybe I'll go with you."

"You're welcome to. Aunt Lou will be pleased."

*****

Greg wanted to ask Janie if it would please her, as well. He couldn't quite figure her out. She seemed happy one moment and serious the next.

He tried not to think about her, but somehow she constantly slipped into his thoughts. He could hardly wait to see what Annabelle and Rich thought of her. Yet he suspected they'd love her on sight.

Twenty minutes across town and Greg pulled up in front of a bungalow. The door opened and a man stepped out. He was a head taller than Greg.

Greg gave him a short wave then opened the other car door for Janie to get out. She slipped out and followed Greg up to the porch. The tall man broke out in a wide grin. "C'mon in. Nice to meet you, Janie. I'm Rich."

Annabelle walked over as they entered the living room. "I'm Annabelle, and this," she patted her stomach, "is either Melissa or Michael." She leaned over and hugged Janie. Janie liked hugs, but usually didn't make the first move. She liked this family already.

"Got the decorations out of the attic," Annabelle continued, "and Rich went after the tree last night."

"Are you feeling better?" Greg asked. "You look the same to me."

Rich laughed. "You can't see the extra pound she's put on?"

"Oh, go on with you," Annabelle said, swatting his arm.

"Let's get started," Rich encouraged. "I'm always in a hurry these days – just in case our baby decides to put in an appearance early."

Annabelle sat on the sidelines giving instructions. "Too many ornaments in the middle section. Put more to the right and left."

The tree had all blue lights and silver ornaments. It looked quite festive. Aunt Lou believed in using all the colors. "More colorful," she'd said.

The decorating proceeded quickly. Janie liked the camaraderie between these people. She hadn't laughed this much in a very long while.

Rich helped Greg with the outdoor lights. They wouldn't let the women come out until it was done. Janie laughed about that. She liked seeing the brothers together. Rich had this enormous laugh that made her laugh, too. She glanced at Greg, thinking she hadn't heard him laugh like that.

*****

Greg didn't need to ask his family what they thought about Janie. She fit right in as if she'd always known them. She laughed along with Annabelle and even laughed at Rich's corny jokes. He'd always been the jokester of the family. *Little brother, who loved hearing laughter.* When they were on the roof, Rich asked about Janie.

"Where did you two meet?"

"I got her out of a ditch."

Rich laughed, his voice carrying across the street and down the block. "You're kidding, right?"

"No." Greg remembered Janie's grin, like a child caught with its hand in the cookie jar. "Fortunately, I gave her my business card."

"Do you usually do that?

"No. Never have before."

"Guess it was a good thing."

Greg grimaced. "Especially when she drove into a ditch an hour later, closer to town."

"What?" Rich stared at him. "She's a klutz?"

"No, just not used to driving in snow."

Rich chortled so hard Annabelle came out to see what was happening.

"You can't see the lights yet," Rich admonished. "We're almost finished."

"I thought so. Apple pie coming up," Annabelle sang out.

After slices of apple pie with vanilla ice cream on top, Janie watched both men have second helping. She couldn't eat more, she already felt stuffed like a goose on Thanksgiving.

"I have an idea." Janie's eyes lit up. "I could bring sugar cookies over and we'll frost and decorate them here to take to my Aunt Lou. It would be nice to surprise her. And you could help, Annabelle."

"Sounds great to me." She patted her stomach. "Just think. Next Christmas we'll have a little one to watch the lights go on."

"That will be a wonderful miracle," Janie sighed. She wondered if there was any chance of her ever having a child. Of course, she would have to meet the right man first... Her eyes turned to Greg. He was staring at her, almost in a daze.

"Uhm, we better get going," Janie gulped.

*****

Greg liked having Janie beside him as he drove. He wished the SUV had bench seats so she could move closer, but that might be rushing things. They'd barely met but he found himself wanting to be with her more and more.

It was the craziest thing ever. He hadn't said a word about a relationship, nor had she, yet here he was thinking about her snuggling up close to him.

He was half way to Lou's house when the beeper sounded. Greg stopped and pulled off to the side. "Do you want to ride with me on a call?"

Janie nodded, looking a bit doubtful.

"It could be something simple. At least it's not an accident."

"The snow has melted," Janie said. "I'm sure that's a good thing. I'll come along."

*****

A woman had suffered a heart attack. Janie stayed in the car while Greg hopped out and rushed over to the house and disappeared. Janie watched for a few minutes and saw him come out again walking beside the woman, who was on a stretcher headed towards the ambulance.

It was intriguing to see him at work. She noted that he was speaking to the woman, soothing her the way he had done when Janie had driven into the ditch. She watched to see if he gave the woman his business card, but from what she could see he did not.

Janie leaned back, letting the last few hours flash through her mind. Good times. Pleasant times. After a few more minutes, the car door opened and Greg slipped in beside her. "The medics are taking her to the hospital. Think she might have broken her arm, too, when she fell out of bed."

Janie nodded sympathetically.

He looked closely at her. "Hope you're not too cold. Sorry I had to leave you in the car."

Janie smiled. "Not a problem. I just grabbed the blanket from the back seat."

"Smart girl." He reached over and held her hand. She didn't pull away. His heart soared. Maybe she cared. He so hoped it was true.

"I'm sorry that this call interrupted our time together. I'm filling in for a few of my friends who wanted to go on trips."

"That makes sense." Janie leaned back on the seat and thought about what a great guy Greg really was.

Chapter Five

Janie wanted to invite Greg in, but knew he had other things to do besides escorting her around town. Rescuing her from ditches was more than enough. He walked her to the door. "Saturday we'll go to the Home, if you still want to do that."

"Of course." She hesitated, wishing Greg didn't have to leave. Her heart hadn't returned to normal yet. She was beginning to wonder if it ever would. She stood on the porch and watched him swing back down the walkway and hop into his SUV. He turned and waved. Then Janie stepped into the house.

"How did the afternoon go?" Aunt Lou sat in her favorite recliner/rocker and looked up as Janie moved into the room. The Christmas lights twinkled everywhere and Janie knew there would be a basket of lights in the bathroom. Maybe in each bedroom, too.

Janie tossed her coat and gloves at the end of the couch and sat, trying not to smile.

Her aunt smirked. "Okay. Tell me every last thing you did and said, so I know why you have that Cheshire cat grin."

"Aunt Lou, he is the most wonderful guy I've ever met. I just know something will happen and my bubble will burst."

"Do you really believe God is in charge of your life?"

"You know I do." Janie swung her foot like she did when nervous or anxious. "I thought David was the one – he seemed to fit with me so well."

"God knew he wasn't the right one," Aunt Lou quietly said. "How did you like Greg's family?"

Janie remembered the warm welcome she'd received. "His brother Rich is funny and I felt I'd known Annabelle forever."

Aunt Lou gave a knowing look. "Did they like you?"

"I think so. Greg thought that we bonded."

"That's wonderful. So no more thoughts of David and what might have been."

"You're right, of course." Janie leaned over and hugged her aunt. "David left. The job was over. So, here I am."

"And I'm thankful for that; you have no idea the hours of prayer I put in."

Janie didn't want to think about David anymore. She was finally ready to close that chapter of her life. Even if things didn't work out with Greg, she knew that there would be no more thoughts of what could have been with David.

"I think we should start the baking."

Lou stood. "Was just thinking the same thing. Have some butter out softening up." She paused. "Do you know when you'll see Greg again?"

"We're going on Saturday to the home where his mother lives."

"Home?"

Janie told her what she knew about Greg's mother. They discussed how difficult it must be for Greg and his brother.

"I think it's wonderful for you to go with him." Lou patted her hand. "That's what Christmas is about; helping others. Spreading the joy."

Janie felt happy that her aunt approved.

"Let's go bake cookies and cupcakes," her aunt's voice rang out cheerfully.

"Cupcakes?" Janie asked. "We've never done that for Christmas before."

"I know, but the Women's Guild is sponsoring a booth at the school carnival and asked for everyone to bake a dozen or so. Cupcakes are so popular right now."

"We can make those fancy, too. I've seen lots of illustrations in magazines." Janie could hardly wait.

"Let's decorate one batch here and you can take one with you to Annabelle's."

Soon endless cupcakes covered one kitchen counter. Cookies were on plates, ready to frost. Decorations filled a plate – chocolate kisses, chips, raisins, colored sugar, chopped nuts and coconut. Then there were the frostings colored red, green and blue.

"I think Annabelle would like this," Janie said, popping a warm cookie into her mouth.

After putting cupcakes into boxes and covering the trays full of cookies, Lou suggested dinner. "Something simple like leftovers."

Janie was biting into a chicken wing when the doorbell sounded. She jumped up and hurried to the door.

Greg stood there, grinning, a large box in his hand.

Janie motioned him to enter and it was all she could do to restrain herself from hugging him. He stood back and held the box out.

"It isn't a fancy gift or anything."

"What--?"

"Chains. They were in the car, under the seat. I thought I'd found everything."

"Oh." Janie looked puzzled. "I forgot I had these chains. I should have put them on when I hit the first snow."

Greg came in and closed the door. His eyes twinkled.

"Then we wouldn't have met."

The look on his face made Janie tingle.

Lou entered the living room. "We're having leftover chicken; care to join us?"

"I ate a burger a few minutes ago." He didn't want to intrude on their meal.

"Come look at what we baked," Janie said, pulling on his arm.

"I could eat a cookie." Greg laughed and followed Janie. When they reached the kitchen he stood amazed at the array of goodies set out.

"These are cupcakes for a sale at the school carnival." Janie picked out one that wasn't as perfect. "For you."

"I thought we were going to decorate cookies next week," Greg said.

"The baking goes on for several days," Lou explained. "Christmas only comes once a year."

Greg reached over and grabbed a knife from the bowl of green frosting. "Where should I put this?" He leaned over and dabbed it on Janie's nose.

Janie moved back, her mouth falling open. She couldn't believe he had done that. So spontaneously. "I think you need the blue." She grabbed the knife next to that bowl.

"What color do I get?" Lou asked from the table where she sat munching on her chicken.

"Red!" Janie said. "Perfect."

"Who's going to take the picture of us clowns?" Lou asked. She wiped the frosting off.

Janie did not hear her aunt. Greg stared into her eyes, took both her hands and pulled her close. She felt a smile crawl across her face. He stepped back, grabbed two cookies and headed for the door.

"I've got to get going. It's my night to shop."

Janie swallowed her disappointment. How could he look at her in a loving way one minute then change so suddenly?

"I'll see you Saturday?" Janie asked, following Greg into the living room. He stood at the door and nodded.

"Yes, we'll be in touch."

"The lights look wonderful, Lou," he hollered over his shoulder.

He was gone. The room seemed so empty, but then Janie began to doubled up with laughter. He hadn't wiped the frosting off his nose. Would he think of it before getting to the store?

*****

Greg could feel his heart thumping in his chest. He hadn't known until that moment when he had pulled Janie so close how he felt. He was head over heels, crazy for her. Yet he knew she had a boyfriend – there'd been talk about this David more than once. Should he have asked her about him?

He didn't look back at the roof with shining lights – the only one on the block. He couldn't look back. If he did, he'd forget about shopping and find out just what David, whoever he was – meant to Janie.

*****

Saturday came and went with no call from Greg. That evening Janie sat alone. She held Greg's business card in her hand and stared ahead. Why hadn't he called her? Why hadn't she called him? She ran different scenarios through her mind.

Maybe he had to go out on an emergency call or maybe something happened to his mother.

"Don't look so crestfallen," Lou said. "It's not over. I know you think it is, but I say not."

"I'm trembling, Aunt Lou. I can't seem to stop. That night when he was here, I wanted to reach up, pull his face down and kiss him – it was all I could do not to do it."

"I know, I could tell."

119

"Maybe he could tell. Maybe he is just not interested that way."

Aunt Lou rubbed her shoulders, but for once remained silent, however, she kept a constant string of prayers going.

*****

Janie and Lou went to church on Sunday and made more cupcakes and cookies on Monday. One dozen cupcakes were ready to take to Rich and Annabelle's house.

By Friday there was still no call from Greg, nor had he stopped by. Janie knew the love she had hoped he would return was all a figment of her imagination. She stared at the decorated room. She loved the lights in her room and she was still glad that she had come, but now knew she'd return to Seattle the day after Christmas.

The phone rang early Saturday morning. Janie slowly walked over and picked up the receiver. She had no hope that it would be Greg.

"Janie?"

"Yes."

"It's Greg."

"I know." Her mind whirled, as she prepared for what she knew he would say. He wasn't the kind of person who didn't explain things. She did know that about him.

"I've been busy."

"Figured as much."

"Not with the job."

"What do you mean?" She gripped the receiver hard, bracing herself for the inevitable letdown she believed would come. He must have someone else in his life.

"I had to take Annabelle to the hospital one night – or should say morning. Rich couldn't get the car to start. He almost called an ambulance, but called me instead."

"She had the baby? It's all right?"

"No, she didn't. But she gave us a bad scare. Now she's home and must have complete bed rest.- I've been staying here, cooking and tending to things so she'll stay in bed."

Relief swept through Janie and she dropped to a chair. "You should have called." She covered the phone and called out to Aunt Lou. "Annabelle almost had her baby."

Lou came into the room. "So that's what happened. I guess we know what we must do."

"What's that?"

"Tell Greg I'll be over to cook a nice meal for the family. It's what I do best."

"I heard that," Greg said when Janie started to tell him.

"And Annabelle and Rich will be so happy."

"We're coming tomorrow – after church," Lou added.

Greg said nothing for a moment. "Do you still want to go to the Home to decorate Mom's room?"

"Yes, of course I do." All thoughts of leaving town were swept from her mind again.

"I'll be there in ten."

When Janie put down the receiver, she turned to Aunt Lou, a huge smile on her face.

"I told you everything would be all right."

*****

"You have your gloves and hat?" Greg asked when Janie answered the door.

She grinned. "I'm ready." She pointed at the boots Auntie had given her. "Though we'll be in the car most of the time."

Greg laughed.

Janie's heart perked up; however, she had decided that she would be more cautious with her feelings. She needed to find out just how Greg felt about her.

Janie was looking forward to meeting Greg's mother, but she worried about how the woman might react.

"Mom won't recognize me," Greg said as they pulled into the parking lot. "She thinks I'm her brother, Ralph."

Janie swallowed the lump that sprang to her throat and looked at his serious expression. She reached for his hand briefly. "It must be difficult."

Greg didn't answer as he reached around and took the garlands and the spray snow. "This is such a good idea, Janie. So glad we're doing it."

They stopped at the desk to sign in. Janie looked around. Lots of people walked the halls; some patients sat in wheelchairs. She couldn't imagine what she'd do if Aunt Lou lost her memory.

"Lunch will be at noon, should you like to stay," the lady behind the desk commented.

"I think not," Greg said. "This won't take long." They made their way down the hall to the next to last room. Greg tapped on the open door before entering. "It's me, Mom. Greg, your son."

A woman with tousled gray hair turned around from where she sat in a wheelchair by the window. An expression of delight crept over her face. A face highlighted with laugh wrinkles around her eyes - eyes so like her son's and filled with awareness that Janie gulped. Relief filled her. This must be one of Mrs. Kinkaid's better days.

"Snow!" Greg's mother said. "It's snowing out. I want to get the sled. Did you bring it, Ralph?"

Janie glanced at Greg to see his reaction. His serious set lips turned into a wide smile.

"No, Mom, didn't bring the sled, but we're going to decorate the room."

"Snow? You brought snow?"

Janie had a sudden idea. She could go out, scoop some up and bring it in. Or, maybe they could take her outside to see it, feel it for herself.

"Can she go outside?"

Greg raised an eyebrow. "I know what you're thinking. Janie, it's a wonderful idea."

Minutes later, after getting permission, Greg wheeled his mother out the front door. The blanket Janie had used after her second accident, draped around the slender woman's shoulders.

"Snow!" she repeated. "Ralph, it's been years since I've been out in the snow."

Greg formed the first snowball and set it in his mother's lap. "Here, Mom, touch it."

She grabbed it and threw it." A snow fight. We can have a snow fight."

Janie formed a snowball and threw it at Greg, He turned with a huge grin on his face

His mother clapped her hands with glee. "I want another one."

Ten minutes later, they wheeled her back inside. All of them had flushed cheeks.

Greg reached for Janie's hand. "You have no idea how much you're coming here with me means. It's all I can do to visit her some days."

His mother's head slumped to the side, as if she were sleepy. Greg helped her into bed and covered her. Her chin quivered and she opened her eyes for a moment. "Snow," she said. "I love the snow."

Greg quickly placed the garlands around the windows and Janie sprayed the fake snow across one window. The room looked much more festive now.

The women in the other bed clapped her hands with enjoyment. "I like you," she said, reaching out to Janie.

Janie hugged her and looked over at Greg's mother. She would sleep for a while. What an adventure they'd had – one she would never forget.

Greg smiled as he picked up the empty decorations sack. This was the first time he had visited his mother that he didn't feel sad.

"It's time to go, Janie." He leaned over and kissed her cheek. "You are special."

Chapter Six

After Greg left her at the front door of Aunt Lou's house, Janie hummed a Christmas tune. "Aunt Lou, he likes me. I know that for sure now."

Lou smiled. "I knew it all along."

An hour later while they both sat and watched *The Christmas Story,* a knock sounded. Greg stood on the porch with a huge poinsettia, a smile on his face.

"I couldn't wait," he said, handing the plant over to Lou. He took his cap off and shook the snow off. "In case you didn't know, it started snowing a few minutes ago."

"It did?" The women both chorused.

"I bought something else," Greg said. "Something that goes on the arch leading into the kitchen."

"What's that?" Lou asked. "I thought we had every possible decoration known to man."

A mischievous gleam came into his eyes. "Ha! You forgot about this." He held up a sprig of mistletoe. "No home can be without mistletoe."

Janie knew in that moment that she wanted this man in her life forever.

Greg began to move towards the kitchen, but then stopped and turned around. "I had to see you, Janie-needed to see the sparkle in your eyes. I'll fight for you if I have to."

"Fight?" Janie asked. "What do you mean?"

"I heard about someone named David."

Janie's hand flew up to her mouth. "David! He's out of my life, has been for some time now."

"Well, am I in your life now?" Greg's voice quivered with emotion.

Janie flew into his arms and felt him tighten against her. "Yes, you are and I don't think I could ever go on without you in my life. I love being with you," she sobbed against his chest.

"And I feel the same about you." He held his arm up over his head. The mistletoe dangled from his fingers.

Janie smiled and lifted her face. He covered her mouth with his.

After a few moments, they walked to the window and looked out at the wonderful flakes of snow that were covering the ground.

"I will always love snow now, because it was what brought us together," Janie promised.

Greg squeezed her close and Janie rested her head on his shoulder.

Aunt Lou, never one to be idle, blew the small Christmas horn that hung from the branches of the Christmas tree.

"And God said, Amen!"

Made in the USA
San Bernardino, CA
26 November 2014